Mount Faylinn

Wilis' Mound

Forbidden Lake

Oliver's Cabin

THEATER

Conservatory

PROLOGUE

It Begins
Mount Faylinn, New York

Most ballets are all sugar plummy with froth. The one called *Giselle*, not so much. These ballerinas dance high on a twisted mountain deep in a shuddering wood. Veiled in wedding white, they're quite beautiful—timeless, graceful, and all that. Too bad they're dead.

While the brokenhearted souls twirl in a misty blue haze, a strain of their ghost music whirs in the hush of the night. It swirls down highways and onto residential streets, up to the second floor where the older sister sleeps. With a swish of a summer curtain, the hum of the haunted enters her window, left open.

CHAPTER ONE

A Broken Music Box
Westchester, New York

"**K**iki, turn off that music," my sister yells from her bedroom.

I lift my head from the pillow and strain my ears in the dark. "What music?"

Thump. Alison slams her window shut. "Never mind, it was coming from outside."

The hour on my bedside clock is a red blur. I slide on my purple glasses and the lit numbers snap into shape: 5:30 a.m. I toss off my blanket and bolt upright. "Is it time?"

"Yep. Chop, chop." She bangs on my bedroom wall twice for emphasis. "Finish packing or we'll miss the train."

My heart pounds like my ballet teacher's cane. I'm excited but nervous. I'd say I'm *nercited*, but that's not a real word. It's funny how that sounds like nearsighted, which is what I am. No wait, I think I'm farsighted. I always get those two confused. Either way, when your eyeballs aren't shaped right, light hits them at the wrong angle. My vision makes the world unreal—like gazing through windows smudged with a ghostly haze. The only way to clear that haze is to wear thick glasses.

"I don't hear you moving in there," Alison singsongs.

I leap up and gather everything I need for the next three weeks: black leotards, pink tights, ballet slippers, assorted summer clothes, and sneakers. But after I toss them all into my red polka-dot suitcase, the zipper won't close.

Alison pops her head in my room. "You ready, Squeak?"

She loves calling me that, and she can because she's not only my sister, but four years older. She's also a head and neck taller, and since she has a giraffe neck and I have no neck, that's a lot of inches hovering over me. Everyone says she was born with the perfect body for a ballerina. No one says that about me.

"Dad's waiting. Close that suitcase and bring it downstairs." She plants her hands on her hips and purses her pink glossy lips. "Now."

I squash everything in the case, sit on it, and try again. This time, the zipper goes halfway around when one of my leotards catches. "It's stuck."

"Get off. Let me try." While she leans over and struggles with the zipper, she lifts her left leg to a perfect one-hundred-eighty-degree *penché*. No matter what she's doing—even if it's only brushing her teeth—she always finds a way to add a ballet stretch to it.

I copy her pose and raise my leg as high as I can. My sad *penché* only makes it halfway up before drooping back down. "How do you get your leg so high? You're so bendy."

She ignores me, too busy with the zipper problem. "I need something pointy," she says. "Straighten out a paperclip."

I rush to my desk and dump the contents of three pencil cases on the floor. Along with all the pens, markers, and rubber bands, an eye makeup kit falls out. Before I can hide it, she glances my way.

"Hey, what are you doing with my eyeshadow?"

Heat rushes to my face. "It's not yours. I bought it with my allowance." I lift it closer. "See?"

She narrows her mascaraed eyes. "Oh yeah, sorry." She switches her *penché* to the other leg, which rises even higher. "Anyway, Dad's not going to let you wear makeup—unless it's for a recital."

"I was only fooling around with it."

She grins. "So are you an expert now?"

I wrinkle my face. "I have no clue which shade to use. Why was I born with this weird curse?"

"What are you talking about?"

"My two different eye colors."

Alison blinks her normal, same-colored eyes at me. "Don't be so dramatic. Having two different eye colors is not a curse."

"Are you sure?"

"I'm pretty certain." She shoves my clothes down again. "Next time, don't pack so much—and do it the night before like Dad told you."

"I was going to, but then I started drawing and—"

"Never mind. Where's that paperclip?"

"Oh, right." I rummage through all the pencil case stuff.

"Focus. Today's a big day."

I let out an Oscar-worthy sigh. "I'm doomed. Watch me get the worst dancer award."

"Don't be silly. No camp does that." She lowers her leg and kneels by the suitcase.

"At least worst dancer would be an award. If you win any more trophies, we'll have to move to a bigger house. All I ever get are showing-up certificates."

"Trophies aren't everything in life."

"But if I don't improve this summer, I won't move up with my class. I'll never get pointe shoes."

She jiggles the zipper back and forth. "You're still young. Don't worry so much."

"I'm not that young. I'm almost twelve, and that's when you got pointe shoes." I place my feet in first position and point to the huge gap between my knees. "Look how bowlegged I am. I've got mini cowboy legs. How am I supposed to balance on them?"

"Hurry, girls," Dad yells from downstairs. "Breakfast is getting cold."

"We'll be there in a minute," Alison shouts. She pries her blue fingernails in the zipper. "You couldn't find one paperclip in that mess?"

"Nope, sorry." I gather everything from the pencil cases. "Want me to look in your room?"

"Wait. I almost have it." She gives the zipper another hard jerk and frees it. She spins it all the way around, closing the suitcase.

Alison and I thump our suitcases down the steps and rush to the kitchen. The table is set with pancakes, whipped cream, and strawberries—my absolute favorite breakfast of all time. Dad's grinning and wearing Mom's old apron—the lacy ruffled one with pink polka dots. That apron is the reason I love dots so much. After Mom died, we all voted to keep the apron, and not just hidden away in some closet, but out in the kitchen—doing its job. It's a good thing too because if Dad wasn't wearing her apron now, he'd have flour smudged all over his good khakis.

The brochure for our summer dance camp is on the table. It's printed on shimmery paper and addressed to us in sparkly-gold ink. I read it aloud while I eat. "It says here, 'Be aware: Ballets come to life at the Conservatory of Mount Faylinn.' What does that mean?"

Alison's mouth is full of strawberries as she answers. "That's just a slogan someone came up with."

"Don't take it literally, Kiki," Dad says. His teddy-bear brown eyes glint at me.

"What does literally mean again?" I ask.

"When something is true." Dad pours more juice. "Not an exaggeration."

"Then how come Alison's friends always say stuff like, 'I literally laughed my—'"

"Hey." Dad arches his brow. "First of all, no cursing, even if you're quoting. And second—or is that secondly? Anyway, I've never personally seen a body part fall off from laughing too much. Have you?"

"Then why do they say it?" I shoot a mischievous glance at Alison. She ignores me, so I turn back to Dad and fiddle with the brochure. "Why are there drawings of fairies all over the brochure? It's not like we'll be doing the Nutcracker in summer."

"The conservatory is named Mount Faylinn, after the town." Dad points to the map on the back. "Faylinn is an old Celtic word that means fairy kingdom."

Oh. I turn towards my sister. "So even though the school's named after a fairy kingdom, I shouldn't take that literally either? Right, Alison?"

She smirks at me and pulls out her phone. "Hang on, I'm texting Dylan."

Of course. She can't survive two minutes without her beloved boyfriend. I make a face and Dad catches it.

"Play nice, girls. Remember, I want you to look out for each other." He checks the cat wall clock with the bulging ticking eyes. "Miss Kitty says it's time. Up and at 'em."

Alison sighs. "We're not five anymore."

"I know, but that doesn't stop me from worrying about you both."

After we finish with the dishes, Dad grabs our suitcases and heads to the front door. "I'm carrying these to the jeep. Last one out, hit the lights."

Alison turns off the kitchen switch and follows me to the living room. She then hurries past me, stopping at the mirror by the front door as she always does. After she smooths her long blond hair and checks her perfect reflection, she glances back at me.

"What are you standing around for, Squeak?" she asks, concerned.

I scan the room. "I don't want to forget anything."

"Okay, but make it quick, and don't forget the lights." Alison steps out and shuts the door.

I spy my backpack with my art supplies on the sofa and snatch it up. I'd hate to forget that. Besides dancing, I love drawing—especially ballerinas. I wrestle my arms through the backpack's straps, and not one second later, I hear *beeeep, beeeep.* That's Alison, pounding the horn for me to speed it up.

"I hear you," I mumble. "You don't have to wake up the whole neighborhood."

After I flick off the living room lights and the ones in the entryway, everything turns black. Everything, that is, except for a faint silver glow pulsing from the kitchen. Slowly, I head toward it, the weird glow expanding as I get closer. When I enter the kitchen, sprays of silver and gold sparks burst around me. I gasp and jump back. A wild, crackling light show is erupting from something on the table.

Then I see it—the source of all this mayhem. The Mount Faylinn brochure.

I lean in for a closer look, and the glittery letters from our address start to squiggle. I blink. Maybe I need new glasses. I rub my eyes, but when I open them, the gold words continue to squirm. Soon, they rise from the page. My whole body tingles as the script expands and twists into a strange foreign word in the air. It starts with the letter *S.*

As I tilt my head and gape, a silver spark zips past my nose. The spark circles the room and smacks into the china cabinet, rattling the plates. A second later, twinkly ballet music starts playing from inside the cabinet.

I rush over and open the glass door. The crank on Alison's music box is turning, the porcelain ballerina spinning within. But this isn't the song it used to play.

The ballerina picks up speed until it's turning so fast the wooden box starts to vibrate. I pick it up, fumbling to find the off switch. But the box shakes violently from my hands.

"Oh no!" I cry.

The delicate box crashes to the floor and shatters, ballerina and all. I stare at it in horror. Alison loved this music box. Her precious Dylan gave it to her last year. She won't believe my story of how it broke. I can hardly believe it. My chest tightens. She knows I don't like him. She'll blame me for breaking it, and there's no time to glue it back together.

At that moment, the front door opens a crack. With a soft whoosh, the brochure sucks the lights and strange word back into its pages. One last spark remains, and with a grand flourish, rewrites our address in swirly gold lettering.

"You coming, honey?" Dad says, sticking his head around the door. With that, the last spark vanishes. Everything returned to normal so fast, he didn't even notice. How can that be? But the mess on the floor remains, and if he comes in, he won't miss that.

"I'll be right there," I say, my breath catching in my throat.

"Okay, better hurry though." He closes the door.

I exhale in relief. I'll tell Alison about the music box when we return from camp. No sense getting her upset about it now. I grab a broom, and as I start sweeping, something crawls out of the cracked box. From the faint light of the waking sun, I can tell it's a spider—a white one. It's around two inches and so ghostlike, my skin prickles at the sight of it.

I don't like killing bugs—even scary ones. "You're going outside," I say.

The spider's bulging eyes glare at me.

"You heard me." As soon as I say that, the white spider scurries off on its spindly white legs. I chase it with the dustpan, but it disappears under the china cabinet. I give up and sweep the shattered pieces, hiding everything in the fancy silverware drawer we never use.

The jeep's horn beeps long and loud.

I rush to the door but hesitate with my hand on the knob. First those weird lights. Then Alison's music box. And now this spider. All on top of my worries about dance camp. Leaving the house like this creeps me out.

I take a breath, and as I hurry toward those three weeks away from home, Dad's pancakes churn in my stomach.

CHAPTER TWO

The MacAdoodle Express

I climb into the jeep, waiting for Dad to mention those crazy lights. But he never says a word. Instead, he turns on the radio and listens to traffic and weather reports. That settles it. I push all those brochure lights out of my mind and blame my nervous imagination.

But what about that creepy spider and Alison's cracked ballerina? I can't blame them on my imagination. My fingers still tingle from that vibrating music box. A wave of guilt rushes over me. Maybe I should confess. But none of it is my fault. I bite my lip as we head to the station.

The rising sun blinds Dad when he turns onto a new road, and he quickly shields his eyes. "Wow, that's brutal," he says and flips down the windshield visor.

He's concentrating on driving—not an ideal time to tell him. I glance over at Alison. She's wearing her headphones, lost in her own world. Her birthday is coming up soon. If Dylan gets her something new, that broken music box won't matter as much. There's no reason to ruin her day. It's not a life or death thing. Plus, that spider should be long gone by the time we get back.

While Alison taps to her music, I take in the glow of the summer morning—before real life starts. I'm quiet so I can hear what the new day wants to tell me. Mom used to say everything in nature has something special to teach us.

In this moment, everything does seem magical. The world is fresh and dewy. Thinking about Mom calms my worries and makes me feel all *lubbly jubbly*. She used to say those silly words whenever something made her super happy inside, like when she'd hug Alison and me.

Before I know it, we reach the train station. While we wait outside on the platform, Dad's forehead gets wrinkly and he pulls out his phone.

"I've changed my mind," he says. "I'm canceling my work trip to drive you up there."

Alison touches his arm. "Mila and her mother are getting on at the next stop. We'll be fine."

"Yes, but—"

"No buts, Dad," Alison says. "We know how much you've missed getting out into the field. You haven't gone on a fossil dig since Mom died."

"I hate that I'll be away for your birthday, Alison. Sixteen is a big one."

"We'll celebrate it when we all get back. You can get me something extra special from Australia—how's that?"

Dad shakes his head. "I don't know. I have a bad feeling."

"Everything's arranged," Alison says, repeating the plan all three of us know. "Someone from the conservatory will meet us when we get off. Mila went last summer and said they're very strict. We won't have time to get in any monkey business. It's all ballet, ballet, ballet."

"I thought Mila wasn't speaking to you," I say before I can stop myself. *Whoops.*

Dad turns to Alison. "You two had a disagreement?" He sounds surprised, which isn't surprising. Alison and Mila have been thick as thieves, as he likes to say, since middle school.

"It's okay now." Alison lowers her gaze and elbows me.

An awkward silence hangs in the air. As usual, Dad looks at me to fill it.

"Mila got jealous when Alison danced the solo in the spring recital," I blurt out. I look everywhere but at him and Alison.

"Well," Dad says to Alison, "I'm glad you two sorted it out. It's hard parting ways with someone you care about."

I tug his arm and attempt to change the subject. "Can you bring home some Neanderthal bones from the Outback? I want to see if people had tiny legs back then."

Dad's thick eyebrows squeeze together. "Sounds like you both want to get rid of me."

"We love you, Dad, and we want you to be happy." Alison gives him a hug and I join in.

"You sure you'll be okay without me?" he asks.

"Hey, Alison!" a voice calls from farther down the platform.

We all turn. It's Dylan, sauntering toward her. He always dresses like he's in a boy band, which means his pants never quite fit. Today, he's sporting skinny black jeans and a thick knit beanie. He waves to Dad and me as an afterthought.

I want to scream, *Hey Dylan, enough with the winter hats! It's the middle of summer!*

But Alison's all *in love,* and her eyes widen at the sight of him. While she rushes to give her too-cool dude a kiss, Dad whispers to me, "Something about that kid rubs me the wrong way."

I nod. "Don't worry, he's not coming. He hates ballet."

I strain my ears to eavesdrop on them because, let's face it, sometimes I'm nosy. Dylan tells Alison she's ruining his summer. I can't hear what Alison says back, but she's waving her arms around a lot like she's trying to make a point.

A few minutes later, the train screeches into our station. After Dad gives us one last hug, Alison and I climb in as Dylan storms off the platform. Alison lets me have the window seat, and as the train jolts and chugs away, we lean out the window and wave goodbye.

Dad's standing there alone with a nervous smile. He blows us a kiss and makes the heart sign with his hands. I miss him and home already.

When our train reaches the next stop, Alison and I peer out to look for Mila and her mother. From our window's view, the only person on the platform is a crooked old woman. After she climbs onboard, our train puffs and squeals away.

"Maybe they got on at a different part of the platform," Alison says. "Wait here while I look for them—and don't talk to anyone while I'm gone." She heads to the door connected to the next car, slides it open, and disappears.

I lean forward and watch the doorway the whole time she's gone. A few minutes later, I catch sight of Alison. She's stuck between the two cars, struggling to open our door. I run over and yank the handle from my side. It finally flings open and a gust of wind swooshes in with her. While we struggle to bang the door shut, Alison's long blond hair swirls and sparkles in the air like she's a video star. My wavy, shoulder-length auburn hair only slaps me across the face. Mom used to say that our hair held the colors of the seasons in which we were born: Alison's, the yellow golds of summer, and mine, the reddish browns of autumn.

"Good teamwork, Squeak," she says, but she's not smiling.

"Thanks," I say as we return to our seats. "Did you find them?"

"They're not on this train. I'd better text Mila." Alison's thumbs type with a furious speed and a moment later, the phone buzzes with a reply.

Alison stares at her phone. "She's not coming."

"Why not?"

Alison's forehead wrinkles. "She broke her leg yesterday playing soccer."

"Since when has Mila played soccer?"

"She was just fooling around at the park with some friends." Alison picks at her blue nail polish. When she does that, I know she's worried.

"We should call Dad."

"No." Alison puts her phone away. "He's on his way to the airport by now."

"But he'll get mad if he finds out we're on the train alone."

"I'm not ruining his trip. Nothing's going to happen to us—it's only a three-hour ride."

The connecting door blows open, admitting a tall, bony man. Dressed in an old-fashioned grey suit and shirt, he heads through the train and sits across from us. A ghost of a smile crosses his lips as he peers in our direction. "Dollars to cobwebs, you girls are heading to the Dance Conservatory of Mount Faylinn."

"How did you know?" I ask meekly.

His long thin finger points to Alison. "She looks like a ballerina."

I nod. "Everyone always—"

Alison grabs my arm and yanks me out of my seat. While she drags me down the aisle, she whispers, "How many times have I told you not to talk to strangers? We're changing seats."

I follow her through the connecting trains, jumping across the swaying metal floor connectors. It's scary but fun. If I combine that, I get *fary*—almost like fairy.

"What's dollars to cobwebs mean?" I yell because of all the clanking and swirling wind between the cars.

"Just be careful and keep moving," she yells back.

I continue following her all the way to the first car. It's crammed with passengers, but we're lucky and find two seats together.

"Oh no." Alison glances back. "I forgot our suitcases. They're still on the rack by that creep."

I frown. "I wanted to draw. I brought all my colored pencils and sketchpads. Can we go back?"

"Tickets. Tickets, please." The conductor bounds into our car singing his announcement. He glances at our tickets and booms out, "You two MacAdoodles headed to Faylinn?"

A passenger in the back laughs.

Alison groans. "It's MacAdoo, not MacAdoodle."

"My apologies." His fuzzy caterpillar mustache rises as he grins. "Did you girls change seats? I thought I saw you get on the last car."

I point to Alison. "My sister made us because—"

Alison kicks me. "The view is better here," she says. "But we forgot our suitcases. One is red with polka dots and the other is light blue. Do you think you could—"

"No problem. I'd be happy to retrieve your luggage." He punches our tickets and slips them in the seat pocket in front of us.

He starts to head off, but Alison stops him, her forehead creased with worry. "Wait, you said our tickets are for Faylinn, but we need to go to *Mount* Faylinn."

He gives us a reassuring smile. "There's no station on the mountain, Miss MacAdoo. Faylinn's the nearest town."

As soon as he's out of earshot, Alison whispers, "If I become a famous prima ballerina I'm changing my name. What do you think of Alison Skye? Or maybe Alison Diamond?"

I burst out laughing.

"Stop it, I'm serious."

"You can't change your name," I say.

"Why not?"

"Because then you're not you anymore. And what would Dad think?"

"Never mind," she huffs.

After he returns with our suitcases, I settle in with my sketchpad and draw ballerinas wearing fancy tutus. I love coloring in their costumes, but their hands always come out looking like claws. I glance over at Alison to see if she can fix them, but she's staring at her phone making a face.

She sees me looking at her and sighs. "Dylan's not answering my texts."

"Maybe he's stuck in traffic, or at the dentist's office, or in a spaceship hurtling to Mars, or—"

"Or maybe he just doesn't care."

Great. There goes any hope of sister-fun—thanks to her beanie-headed, mood-zapper boyfriend. "He did come to see you off," I say, trying to sound upbeat.

She tilts her head and picks off more blue polish. I bet she's adding and subtracting his caring points.

"You're right," she says. "He did get up really early. Maybe he went back home and fell asleep."

I'm glad that's solved for now. I hope when I'm her age, I don't get hypnotized by some boy like Dylan. I've got too many things I want to conquer. First, there's my whole pointe shoe obsession thing. They're so pink and shiny and they make ballerinas look like they're dancing on air. But if I don't improve my balance and leg strength, I'll never get them. Second, I want to master a triple *pirouette*. I can hardly do a decent single. Third, my *arabesque* is droopy. I could go on and on. In dance, there are a million things to work on. I can't even think about them all without freezing my brain, so I go back to drawing and try to fix those hideous claw hands. I can't even draw a decent ballerina.

"How's little Miss Degas doing? You know who he was, right?" Alison always likes to teach me stuff.

"Yes, I know. But I'll never paint ballerinas like he did. Can you help me?"

"Me? You draw better than I do. Just keep at it." She pauses. "I was just thinking. Dylan is a great artist. Maybe he could give you some lessons."

I'd rather draw monster hands for the rest of my life, but I don't say that. Instead, I take out a fresh sheet of paper and sketch my own left hand over and over. Then I practice drawing Alison's right hand in all different positions. I only take a break to eat one of the peanut butter and jelly sandwiches we packed. By the time we approach our station, I've erased my drawings so many times, there are holes where the dancer's hands should be.

"Faylinn, next stop." The conductor hurries through our car, pointing to us.

Brakes squealing, the train clanks into the station. "This is it," Alison says, jumping to her feet. "Grab your suitcase and stay close to me."

CHAPTER THREE

The Tall Stranger Leads the Way

I take a deep breath and follow Alison down the train steps. The summer air upstate is crisp and clean like a snowy day—but warmer and without the snow. Alison and I hold our suitcases and glance down the platform. No bus or taxi is waiting for us. The only person in sight is the grey man exiting from the train. Alison turns back to speak to the conductor, but he's already popped his head inside the train like a turtle. The doors shut and the train hisses and speeds away.

The tall man moseys toward us, holding a clipboard. "If you young ladies are Alison and Kiki MacAdoo, then I'm your driver. How was your trip from 8 Buttercup Lane?"

"You know where we live?" I blurt out.

Alison darts her eyes at me.

"If you're headed to Mount Faylinn, I do. I addressed every brochure myself. Yours was the last, and wouldn't you know it, my pen ran out of ink. It was too late to drive to town, so I thought, why not use my special occasion ink?" His eyes glisten and he flashes a peculiar smile. "It's magical, you know."

My breath hitches. "Magical how?"

Alison glances from side to side, shifting her feet.

"That gold ink was given to me many years ago. And you know the old saying, 'Get a gift, give a gift.'"

I glare at him with my mouth open. I've never heard of that saying.

Alison tightens her lips and grabs my hand.

"Well then." He clears his throat. "Shall we go?" He points across the street to an old wooden station wagon. "There's your chariot to the Conservatory of Mount Faylinn." He swirls his arm and bows. "At your service."

Alison tugs me a step back from him. I think she's planning for us to make a run for it.

"One moment. There's something wrong here." The man stares at his clipboard, scratching his head. "I'm supposed to pick up four people from this train. I've got two more names here—a mother and daughter from 13 Shadow Road."

I nod. "That's Mila and her mom. They're not coming. Mila broke her leg."

Alison tightens her grip on my hand.

"Pity. I guess it's just us." He reaches out his arm. "I can carry those bags for you."

"Wait." Alison pulls out her phone. "I'm checking with the school first."

"Aye, that's smart of you. Go ahead," he says, nodding.

"What's your name?" Alison asks while waiting for the call to connect.

"Did I forget to introduce myself? So sorry. I'm Jeremiah Crumb. My family goes back four generations around these parts." He crosses his arms.

Someone answers Alison's call, and she explains the situation. "Okay, uh-huh, thanks." When she hangs up, she nods.

"All right then, shall we go?" He motions to his station wagon.

Alison still doesn't move. "If your car's here, why were you on the train with us?"

"I was in the city looking into some new lights and props for our theater. My '54 Bel Air's a workhorse, but I'm not pushing my luck driving her that far."

Alison hesitates. She then nods at me, and we follow him across the street to his station wagon. While he loads our luggage, we settle into the back seat. As he drives off, I crank down the window and take in the local scenery. First, we pass a little town lined with cute shops with colorful awnings. Beyond that, the road opens up to cornfields and pastures dotted with apple-red farmhouses. In the distance, a tree covered mountain looms.

After a few more miles, evergreens grow dense. To my right, a wooden sign states in faded black letters: *Mount Faylinn—Dead Ahead.* Soon our road narrows and starts to climb. The station wagon curls up the edge of the mountain and my right ear pops. I try holding my nose and blowing air out of my ears. That only makes it worse, so I stick my finger inside my ear and jiggle it.

Alison glances up from her phone. "What are you doing? It's annoying."

"My ears are popping."

"That's from the change in air pressure," Jeremiah says. "Swallow a few times."

I gulp and it works. "Thanks."

Alison shakes her head and goes back to her precious cell.

"We're almost there." Jeremiah points up. "The conservatory is at the top of Mount Faylinn." He lowers his voice, "Some say it's surrounded by a magical forest." He sounds as serious as he was on the train.

I perk up. "What do you mean?"

His deep-set eyes reflected in the rearview mirror catch mine. "One must always exercise caution around these

parts. As in life, we confront all kinds—from good to evil."
He abruptly stops talking and his forehead creases.

I don't know what to say. First a magical brochure, and
now the whole forest? I peer at Alison for her reaction, but
she's immersed in her own world. Either she didn't hear
what he said, or she thinks he's full of baloney.

When we reach the top of the mountain, the road is
blocked by a black iron gate. Jeremiah steps out of the
wagon and inserts a skeleton key into its lock. While he
struggles to push it open, I read the engraved stone sign set
next to it: *Dance Conservatory of Mount Faylinn, established 1907.*

The gate squeals open. "Those old hinges could use a
bit of grease," he says as he climbs back in the wagon. He
picks up his clipboard and glances at it. "A few more students are due to arrive. I might as well leave the gate open
for now."

We drive through and continue along a paved stone
road that slithers through a forest of pines. Scattered
throughout the woods, pinprick lights blink at us like tiny
watching eyes. I glance over at Alison again, but her head's
still down.

"There she sits, ladies." Jeremiah points to a huge castle-like building with turrets rising from the forest.

Alison finally glances up. "It looks medieval."

Jeremiah nods. "Notice the limestone and crisscrossed
timbers? Madame Valinsky loved the Tudor style. She had
it built to her specifications at the turn of the century."

"The 1990s?" I ask.

Jeremiah grins. "No, my dear. The other century—
1897. It took ten years to build. It was a present from her
husband as a grand gesture of his love."

As we approach the conservatory, Alison leans forward. "Look," she says, touching my arm. "That bronze
statue—in the middle of the circular drive. Recognize it?"

My mouth drops. "That's the Little Dancer by Degas! It must be worth billions!"

Alison shakes her head and laughs. "Don't get so excited. It can't be the real one."

Jeremiah nods. "That one is on display in a museum in Washington, D.C. There are actually twenty-eight authorized replicas in museums all over the world. But alas, this is not one of them. Madame Valinsky hired a sculptor to copy it. Did you know the model was only fourteen? Some say her expression depicts her forced confidence."

"What happened to her?" I ask.

"Sad story," he says, shaking his head. "She was late too many times and the Paris Opera Ballet dismissed her."

"They kicked her out?" My eyes grow wide with shock.

Jeremiah nods.

I stare at the statue. *Poor girl. I bet she tried as hard as she could.*

Jeremiah veers the station wagon to a gravel lot to the right of the circle and parks. After he removes our suitcases, we follow him along the stone path to the front of the conservatory.

"That Madame Valinsky... was she a dance teacher?" I ask.

Jeremiah shakes his head. "She contracted polio when she was a child. It left her crippled and confined to a wheelchair. But she and her husband had a lovely daughter named Priscilla. They say when Priscilla was little, she never walked if she could dance. She twirled and leapt across all the huge rooms. She even danced in the pastures and woods. When she turned seven, her parents hired a dance teacher who traveled all the way from Russia to instruct her. Soon after, they opened the mansion to other students as well."

"Did Priscilla become a famous ballerina?" Alison asks.

"No." Jeremiah opens the arched front door. "It was tragic what happened. She—"

A tall, willowy woman in flowing black scarves appears at the door, her platinum-grey hair pulled in a tight bun. "Hello, my young dancers," she says with a slight French accent.

"These are your new charges, Madame Dupree. May I introduce Alison and Kiki MacAdoo."

I'm not sure if I should curtsy, so I just wave.

Madame Dupree narrows her eyes and tilts her head as she studies us. "I hope your trip here was a pleasant one. Jeremiah, please take Alison's case to room twenty-seven and Kiki's to room thirty-seven. Girls, you may follow me into the parlor."

Madame Dupree glides through the entryway with the grace of a swan, and I waddle behind like a little duckling. As we move down a long hall checkered in shiny black and white tiles, I study a series of dioramas adorning the dark paneled walls. Each one depicts a different ballet featuring intricately painted cardboard cutouts of dancers and scenery.

"Do you like them?" Madame Dupree asks.

I nod. "They're beautiful."

A smile creases her lips. "I did them many years ago. But I can't work a scissor or tiny brush the way I used to." She raises her bent fingers. "Arthritis." She then swings open a pair of carved doors. Inside, tall stained-glass windows paint the parlor with a crimson glow. She motions for us to sit on a velvet couch across from a massive stone fireplace.

"Placement classes begin tomorrow after breakfast. We will group you according to ability. I will explain all the conservatory's rules in the theater at four o'clock today during a general assembly. After that, dinner will be served in the dining hall at six o'clock." Madame Dupree presses an intercom buzzer on the wall and a few moments later, a short woman in a maid's uniform appears.

"Hazel, please show these dancers the location of the library, the dining hall, the rec room, and theater, and then take them to their rooms—twenty-seven for Alison here, and thirty-seven for Kiki. I will see you girls later."

As soon as Madame Dupree is out of earshot, Hazel whispers, "Just so you know, girls, my name isn't Hazel."

Alison shoots her a confused look and says, "I don't under—"

"My name is Louise. Our Madame Dupree is, shall we say, a bit up in the years and getting a wee forgetful. Lately, she's been calling me the name of a character from an old TV show. I think it was about a maid named Hazel. But don't worry, it's only little things she's starting to forget. She remembers everything there is to know about ballet." Louise holds open a door for us. "Anyway, come with me. This is a very large mansion, and it's easy to get lost."

After Louise shows us the dining hall, rec room, and library, she opens a back door and points to a winding stone pathway that splits a garden before continuing into the forest. "The theater's in a separate building, just down that way to the left. You can't miss it. A bell will sound at four to remind you about the assembly."

In the garden, some students are sitting on a bench reading. A few of the younger ones dart around trees and benches, playing tag.

"Alrighty then." Louise shuts the back door. "Time to climb all those stairs to your rooms."

When we reach room twenty-seven on the second floor, Louise opens an old paneled door and motions Alison to enter. I peek inside, and the scent of lilac fills my nose. The spacious room is grandmotherly with old dressers and faded flowered wallpaper.

"Your roommate hasn't arrived yet." Louise points to the twin beds with iron headboards. "Pick out whichever one you'd prefer, but remember to save half the drawers and closet."

"I like it." Alison glances around. "It's homey."

"Okay, Kiki, you're next," Louise says.

Alison turns to me and gives me a quick hug. "You okay?"

I nod, but after she shuts the door, I get teary-eyed. I know I'll see her in a little while, but I still wish we could room together.

"Don't worry, dear," Louise says. "You have a very nice roommate waiting to meet you. Come along now. You're directly above your sister."

Louise huffs as we climb to the third floor. "Here you are—room thirty-seven." Louise knocks first and then opens the door.

Inside, a cocoa-haired girl is on the floor, stretching her legs in a straddle split as she reads. She glances up as we enter.

"Hi there," she says. Her green eyes glisten like a summer lake.

"Kiki, meet your roommate, Suzie." Louise ushers me further inside. "I'll be leaving now, and don't forget—general assembly at four." The door clicks shut behind her.

"I'm from Orlando." Suzie grins. "What about you?"

"Wow," I say. "You came that far? I live closer—in Westchester."

"Florida's brutal in the summer. My parents thought mountain air would be a nice change for me." Suzie springs up and heads to the closet. "Jeremiah left your suitcase in there. I made sure to save half the hangers for you."

I like her right away. She helps me unpack and before we know it, the four o'clock gong rings.

CHAPTER
FOUR

The Warning

Suzie and I hurry down the stairs and out the back door toward the theater. Around seventy other girls, from eight to sixteen years old, have gathered in front. I glance around for my sister. A few moments later, she arrives, talking with a group of girls her own age. Before I can motion to her, Madame Dupree appears and opens the arched blue doors to the theater.

"Pick any seat, but do it quickly." Madame Dupree claps her hands. Suzie and I wind up toward the front, while Alison sits way in the back. I turn and she waves at me.

Madame Dupree makes her way onto the stage, and a hush falls over the theater. "I assume you are all here because you love ballet and wish to improve your technique and artistry. If that is not the case, call your parents immediately and have them take you back home. We are here to work."

A murmur travels from row to row. We all crane our necks to see if anyone leaves. No one does. Everyone is either serious about dance or too afraid to move.

"Good. Now I will review the rules."

The auditorium lights flicker, causing a few cries of alarm. There's shuffling as some pull out their cell phones in case they need flashlights.

Madame Dupree is unfazed. "We do not allow cell phones during the week. Bring them to the dining hall at six, where Jeremiah will collect them. We will return them to you on the weekend."

Gasps and groans rise from the auditorium, the flickering forgotten. One of the older girls raises her hand.

Madame Dupree pays her no mind. "Nonnegotiable. I shall continue. Lights out at nine for the younger girls and at ten for the upper division. Pink tights and black leotards only for class. Teens may wear pink or black chiffon ballet skirts and legwarmers. Your parents were informed of this, so don't pretend you did not know. Also, all long hair in a bun. Tomorrow we will run audition classes to decide where to place you."

The lights flicker again. Madame Dupree pauses, her brow wrinkling and lips tightening, but she continues. "Now what I'm going to say next is extremely important. The Conservatory of Mount Faylinn is surrounded by many acres of dense forest. During your time between classes, you are free to enjoy the gardens while it is still daylight. But do not—and I repeat for emphasis—*do not* wander deep into the forest, especially to the other side of the lake. Do you all understand?"

All of the students remain quiet, except for one girl in the back, who yells, "Why can't we go there?"

"Because you may get lost!" Madame Dupree shouts, face reddening. She hesitates and takes a deep breath. "The forest holds its own rules. Nothing acts the way it should. If you go to the other side, you may come back changed—if you come back at all." Suzie and I glance at each other, confused.

I think of what Jeremiah said in the car before slowly raising my hand. Madame Dupree points to me. "I don't understand. Changed how?" I say.

Madame Dupree shakes her head. "Let's move on."

One student calls, "But—"

"I'll put it more simply. You are *forbidden* to go deep into the forest and cross the lake. Camp rules."

A spotlight above Madame Dupree fizzes and then crackles. She glances up. Everyone's eyes follow hers. A second later, the whole auditorium goes black. I think back to the kitchen this morning. I'd almost forgotten about it. Almost.

Suzie clutches my hand. "I hate the dark," she whispers.

A shuffling sound moves across the stage and something rustles. The microphone squeals. I hold my ears.

"Please remain seated." Madame's voice pierces the darkness. "Everything is—" The mic wails again. "Everything is fine. The lights will come back—"

A crash of glass shatters onstage, the sound amplified through the speakers. The whole auditorium gasps. As I hold my breath and wait in the dark, Suzie tightens her death grip on my hand.

Madame Dupree's voice returns to the mic, breathless. "Do not worry. Jeremiah is repairing the lights. They will resume shortly."

A tense minute later, something bangs and all the lights switch on with a whoosh. Madame is still onstage, standing next to broken glass from a shattered spotlight. Jeremiah appears with a broom and sweeps it off stage.

"You are all dismissed for now, children." Madame Dupree waves us off with a shaking hand. "Meet back in the dining hall at six—and don't forget your cell phones."

As the students mill out of the theater, they chatter about the blackout and the forest and lake. I overhear a girl laughing about a "boogeyman" hiding in the woods. I stand on my toes to look for Alison, but she's already disappeared from the crowd with her new friends.

"Sorry I got so freaked out," Suzie says.

"That's okay. It was kind of spooky. But I remember Jeremiah said something about needing new lights."

"I bet the forest is crawling with spiders and snakes." Suzie scrunches her face in disgust. "In Florida, we have all kinds of weird animals. Last week, an alligator walked right onto our deck. My mother and I screamed our lungs out."

As we head to our room on the third floor, Suzie and I talk about more gross things—like the spitballs her brother flings at her with his tongue. But in the back of my mind, I think about what could possibly be so bad in a forest.

When the six o'clock bell rings, Suzie grabs her cell phone and we hurry down the three flights of stairs. The dining hall's stained-glass windows and high-beamed ceiling make it look like an old church. As the students file in, their voices echo in the vast room. Everyone finds a place at the long wooden tables that run the length of the room.

Alison appears and touches my shoulder. "Sit with me, Squeak."

A warm feeling rises inside me. Alison's my piece of home wherever we go. "Can Suzie come too? She's my roommate." I grab Suzie's hand and her face blossoms into a smile.

"Of course." Alison lifts a leg to slide onto a bench and pats the end spots beside her. "I'm glad you found a friend already."

After Suzie and I slide in, Alison gives me one of her concerned looks. "Sorry I missed you in the auditorium.

This must be hard for you—being away from home and all."

"It won't be so scary at night with Suzie in the room."

Suzie grins again.

Alison nods. "Speaking of home, I texted Dad to let him know we arrived okay. I didn't hear back, so I guess he's flying above the ocean now, forty thousand miles high."

"I'm pretty sure that's forty thousand feet, not miles," I say.

"That's what I meant, Miss Smarty Pants."

Bing, bong, bing. The loudspeaker's chimes cut into everyone's chatter. "Attention young ladies and gentlemen."

"We have boys here?" Suzie says.

The three of us glance around the dining hall. At the other end of the long table next to mine, four boys about my age are seated together. The announcement has many of the girls staring in their direction, and three of the boys smile from all the attention. But the fourth dark-haired boy's face turns a blotchy tomato shade.

The announcement continues, "Hazel and Jeremiah will come around the room collecting cell phones." Madame Dupree is still calling Louise the wrong name.

Jeremiah starts at one end of the dining hall, Louise at the other, both carrying plastic tubs, stickers, and markers for each student to label their phone. Before they get to our table, Alison pulls out her phone and checks for any last-minute messages. Her shoulders slump, and after she hands it over, she starts picking at her nail polish. I figure she hasn't heard from Dylan, but I don't want to bring up that dreaded topic.

Suzie gives Jeremiah her phone, and then he turns to me. "Where's yours?"

"I don't have one. My father says I'm too young."

"Your father's right," Jeremiah says. "They didn't have these contraptions back in my day. Timewasters, that's what they are. They don't work in the forest anyway—not where my cabin sits." Then he moves on to the next group of girls.

For dinner, we're served chicken with potatoes, which taste almost as good as Dad's. For dessert, we get a slice of apple pie with a big scoop of chocolate ice cream. Afterward, we all climb upstairs to our rooms. I share my sketch paper with Suzie, and we draw until lights out.

After we turn them off, we joke and laugh in the dark. As I'm about to drift off, I remember tomorrow is audition day for class placement. My heart picks up, pounding like my ballet teacher's cane again. Whenever she bangs out the beats and stares at me, I know she's thinking, *Why can't Kiki hear the music—and what the heck are those feet doing?*

After that, my nerves kick in. I can't sleep. I miss Dad, our house, and my room. I glance over at Suzie, who is already dreaming.

Outside, the night world clings to the bedroom window. From high in the starless sky, a sliver of a moon casts a blue beam across my blanket. A crisp wind rushes in the open window. Suzie shivers in her sleep. Somehow, she's knocked off her covers. She must be freezing. I'm sure kids from Florida aren't used to cold mountain breezes. I climb out of bed, tuck her back in, and head to the window to shut it. From somewhere in the trees, wind chimes tinkle. They sound like tiny doll bells.

Outside, something flitters past. A moth?

A second later, another shoots past. It shimmers with a flickering blue light. Not a moth. A firefly maybe?

I squint to get a better look. From what I can tell without my glasses, they look larger than fireflies, and more willowy—and more see-through, almost sheer. As I breathe

the cool air, another phantom-blue light drifts past. Soon more appear, all floating to the window below mine.

Wait. Louise said my room was directly above my sister's. I gasp. That's Alison's window. At least twenty lights hover there, flickering like candlelight. I squint harder. One of the lights looks almost like a tiny person wearing a filmy tapered dress. Like a fairy.

I close my eyes. A *fairy?*

When I reopen my eyes, the fairy figure is still suspended with the other lights, glimmering a bright sapphire-blue. Goose bumps rise on my neck and arms.

I run to Suzie's bed and shake her. "Wake up, you have to see this!"

She mumbles something.

"Hurry!" I whisper.

Her eyes slit open. "It's morning already?"

"No, but look outside." I grab her arm. "There's... something!"

By the time we reach the window, the glowing lights are gone.

"What's going on?" she asks, yawning.

"You wouldn't believe what I saw." I motion my hands in the shape of the cloud of lights and realize I look like a crazy person. "There were these fireflies, but maybe they weren't? I mean, they didn't look at all like bugs, and then there were flickering blue lights everywhere." I'm speed talking. "It was almost like a... like a fairy or something."

Suzie looks carefully at me. "Where are your glasses?"

I gesture at my nightstand table. "So?"

"So, you're not wearing them."

"Yeah, but—"

"I'm sure they were just fireflies," Suzie says, holding back a yawn as she climbs into bed. "Tomorrow's an important day. We really need to rest. You don't want to mess up during the auditions, do you?"

"Look, I know this is crazy. But this thing happened at my house this morning—"

Suzie's already asleep.

CHAPTER
FIVE

The Dreaded *Pirouettes*

During breakfast, Alison, Suzie, and I sit together again. While Suzie and Alison chow down the French toast, I don't eat a thing. I'm still thinking about last night and those strange blue lights outside Alison's window. I wait for her to mention them, but she doesn't. On top of that, my stomach is twisted in a pretzel because of what's coming next.

After breakfast, we change into our leotards and tights and head to the dance rooms. Alison waves as she runs off with the older division, while Suzie and I go in the other direction with the eight- to twelve-year-olds. The studio is lined with barres and mirrors like the one back home, but this room is much larger, with maple floors and arched windows.

Madame Dupree is sitting in a red director's chair at the far end. She nods as we enter. "I am here today only to observe." She's holding a spiral notebook and a pink pen with poufy feathers on top. I'm afraid once she sees me in action, that poufy pink pen will take great joy in writing, *"Kiki MacAdoo is a horrible dancer—the absolute worst."*

"Good morning, everyone." A lanky woman in a periwinkle ballet skirt glides into the room. With her blond hair pulled into a bun and her willowy limbs, she reminds me of the ballerinas from my coloring books. All eyes fixate on her as she heads to the stereo and places her leather dance bag on a folding chair.

She pulls out her CDs and notes. "My name is Miss Genevieve."

Madame Dupree nods to her and stands. "Miss Genevieve will be working with you today. Just a reminder before we start: no gum chewing and no talking during class."

One of the younger girls runs over to the wastebasket and spits out a wad of gum.

Miss Genevieve smiles and claps her hands. "Now, please find a place at the barre."

My stomach flutters like a big old crow is trapped inside. I swallow and hurry to the spot next to Suzie. Miss Genevieve stands in the center of the room and demonstrates a pattern of *pliés* and *relevés*—where we bend our knees, straighten them, and rise to half toe.

"Does everyone have that?" she asks.

Most of the girls nod, but I've already forgotten half of it.

"Good. Then we shall begin. Left hand on the barre." The music starts and I recognize it as one of Chopin's piano pieces.

Miss Genevieve calls out the movements as we go through all the positions on both sides. Next, we move on to exercises that involve pointing, circling, brushing, and stretching our legs. I get lost with some of the patterns, but I follow Suzie, who is in front of me on the left side. She has an amazing memory for steps. The only problem is whenever we switch to the right. The little girl in front of me with the popsicle-orange hair is as lost as I am.

After we finish at the barre and with our leg stretches, we move across the floor on a diagonal. My turns to the right aren't too bad, but when I go left, that's a whole other story. My left leg isn't as smart as my right. I feel bad for it because I know it's trying. Some of the other girls get fancy and throw in doubles to score extra points. But by the looks of it, I'm not the only one who can't turn well. By the time we finish all that spinning, the poor little orange-haired girl has to sit on the floor—she's dizzy and nauseated. I hope she keeps her French toast down. Last year, a girl in my class lost her breakfast while turning across the floor. Talk about gross. I'll have to remember to tell Suzie about that one later.

When it's time for *grand jeté* leaps, I point my foot for preparation and take a deep breath. While I run three steps and throw my legs up into a leaping split, I watch my reflection. Horrible. I peek over at Madame Dupree, who is whispering something to Miss Genevieve. Some of the girls have perfect splits high in the air, and a few others can even extend their legs above 180 degrees. Mine look like short wimpy noodles in comparison.

We finish the class by learning a combination facing the mirror. My heart pounds. I know these steps—we do them at my dance school all the time. The problem is the part with the dreaded *pirouettes*—turns done in place. Miss Genevieve splits us into three groups, and since I'm in the third one, I get a momentary reprieve. My legs weaken while I wait, and I hold on to the barre to steady myself.

Miss Genevieve picks Suzie for the first group and places her in the center. I notice the popsicle-haired girl, who thank goodness hasn't barfed yet, is in my group. I know what that means—the first group is the cream of the crop. Now it's my stomach that churns while I wait and watch. As the fast waltz starts, Miss Genevieve gives group one a count of six to start. It plays out exactly as I feared—Suzie and the rest of this group execute perfect *pirouettes*. The least anyone does is a double. Suzie and some of the girls do triples and quadruples. Madame Dupree's pink puffy pen scribbles away.

When it's my group's turn, my mouth goes dry. As I head to the center of the room, my legs can hardly hold me. After Miss Genevieve calls out the starting counts, some of the girls go the wrong way and bang into each other. Miss Genevieve stops the music and reviews the steps a few more times. But even after my group gets the hang of the steps, the *pirouettes* remain a disaster—mine included. I'm doomed. I know it.

At the end of the class, we clap for our teacher—it's ballet tradition. Miss Genevieve smiles and thanks us. Madame Dupree tells us to check the bulletin board in the parlor at five o'clock for our class placements.

As we file out into the hall, Suzie runs over to me. "I hope we'll be in the same class," she says.

"Me too." I lower my head. "But I know I'm not as good as you."

Suzie grabs my hand. "I can't do everything good," she says. "My jumps are lousy. I was lucky we didn't do them today. I can't do more than an *entrechat quatre*. Everybody's good at different things. That's what my mother always tells me and my brother."

I can't even remember what that step is, but I don't tell her that. Down at the end of the hall, an older class is getting out. I see Alison heading for me.

"How'd it go, Squeak?" she asks.

"As expected," I say.

"I'm sure you did fine." She pats me on the back. "I've got to run to a pointe class, but I'll catch you at lunch."

My group has a lyrical class next, which is kind of like ballet but more modern. You practice acting out different emotions and work on your facial expressions. Sometimes you have to pretend you're happy, but other times you have to think of something tragic. It depends on the music. The teacher's name is Miss Sandy. Like her name, her hair is the color of sand tinged with eggplant-purple streaks.

There's no pressure during this class since Madame Dupree's not in the room. I'm sure she's already made her mind up from the ballet class. The hour flies by and before I know it, the lunch bell rings.

While we eat, Alison chatters away about her pointe class. She's excited because after lunch, her teacher is taking her class to a ballet shop in Faylinn. Some of the teens need to pick out new pointe shoes, Alison included. Her shoes never fit quite right and give her blisters.

I'm happy for her but wish I were getting pointe shoes also. I don't care how much they hurt. Even though I know I'm not ready for my own pair, I'd still love to see the shop and watch the girls get fitted.

Suzie's eyes widen. "I overheard a student say a witch owns that shop. But even if she does, it would be neat to go—not alone of course."

"A witch?" Alison laughs so hard, she almost chokes on her drink. "I think she's just old."

A ballet shop—possibly run by a witch? Now I *have* to go. I beg Alison to ask if Suzie and I can come along. At first, Alison shakes her head; she doesn't want to bother the teacher. But after I bug Alison some more, she says that she'll see.

CHAPTER
SIX

A Perfect Fit

After lunch, Suzie and I run up to the third floor to our room and change into our regular clothes. We hurry down to the lobby and wait near Alison's group with our fingers crossed. When Alison's teacher, Miss Natalia enters, I tug on Alison's shirt and give her my puppy dog look.

"Please?" I beg. "Pretty please with a chocolate cherry on top?"

"Oh, all right," Alison says. "I'll go over and ask her."

Along with our fingers, Suzie and I cross our arms, our legs and toes. A moment later, Alison gives us the thumbs up.

I run over and give her a big kiss on the cheek. "Lubbly jubbly."

"What?" Suzie gives me a *you're weird* look.

Alison smiles. "It's a British expression. Our mother used to say it when something made her happy."

"The bus is here," one of the students announces.

We all rush out as Jeremiah pulls up to the front in a regular school bus painted purple. Suzie grins at me and we climb in with Alison and the nine other girls from her pointe class. The teens shoot us confused looks until Miss Natalia explains we're only coming for the ride. After we all buckle up, Jeremiah steers away from the school and down the twirling mountain.

This time, it's Suzie's ears that pop from the change of air pressure. After I tell her to swallow, she starts gulping away, making crazy contorted faces. Once I start giggling, she keeps making faces even after her ears get sorted out. That is until Alison turns around from her seat and shoots me a *knock it off* look. The one that says, *You're lucky to be with the older girls—quit embarrassing me.*

Jeremiah drops us off on Main Street in Faylinn, and we all follow Miss Natalia down a narrow, slanted side street called Praity Lane. All the shops are in cream-colored buildings with dark wooden beams. After we pass a hat store, a cheese shop, and a yarn store, we reach the Coppelia Ballet Shoppe at the end of the lane. It looks ancient.

Suzie tilts her head. "Does this building seem crooked? Or is it me?"

We both giggle as one of the girls rushes ahead to open the lopsided door. She twists the brass knob, but the door is locked. Miss Natalia tells the girls to be patient, that we must ring the bell. Since Suzie and I are the youngest, she gives us the honors. We each take a turn ringing it, and while we wait, we try to peer inside the diamond-shaped windowpanes. We run from one narrow window to the next, but pink velvet drapes cover every inch of rippled glass.

A few moments later, a bony hand with knobby knuckles pushes the tasseled drapes aside. A frail woman with storm-grey hair peeks out the window. Her keen, deep-set eyes study us behind half-moon glasses. She then nods, and with a clunking sound, unlocks the door.

"Come in," her voice creaks out.

Brass bells hanging from the door jingle as the twelve of us follow Miss Natalia. When I step inside, my eyes widen at the sight of it all. Pointe shoes, leotards, and tutus fill the room. Two stories of shelving reach the high ceiling, with everything bathed in a candle-like glow. The classical music playing is the icing on the cake. I'm in heaven.

"Girls, this is the shopkeeper, Madame Babikov." Miss Natalia bends and kisses her on both cheeks. "She's an expert in fitting toe shoes. She was a ballerina in Russia."

Madame Babikov's thin lips curl. "That was lifetime ago."

She's only an inch or so taller than I am. Since I'm still growing, maybe there's hope for me as a short ballerina after all. But then again, people were much shorter back then, weren't they? Ugh, why couldn't I have been born a hundred years ago?

"I know some of you already have shoes, but I want to make sure they are absolutely right for you," Miss Natalia says. "Everyone's feet are different. Madame Babikov will examine you and decide which shoe is the best fit."

"Back in my days, we do not have such choices." Madame Babikov points to her feet. "These poor *nogi* took terrible beating. Now I must wear the ugly Frankenstein shoes with soles like car tires." She limps toward the fitting chairs and points to all the shelves with her pearl-pink cane. "Now we have oodles of the toe shoes. Shoes for narrow or wide feet, shoes for strong or weak arches, shoes for toes too long or too crooked. Shoes, shoes, shoes everywhere. Somewhere here in shop, the perfect shoe, she waits for you—like Cinderella. When you wear, you dance better than ever."

While Miss Natalia begins to call the girls alphabetically for their fittings, Suzie and I explore the shop. First, we rush to the racks of tutus and slip long pink tulle ones over our street clothes. Then we race over to the velvet shelves displaying rows of crowns. Suzie picks out a gold one encrusted with rubies, while I choose a sparkling rhinestone tiara. After we place them on our heads, we twirl in front of a gold framed mirror until we get dizzy and flop onto a slipper-pink sofa.

Suzie leans in close and whispers, "Do you think Madame Babikov really is a witch?"

Before I can answer, Alison rushes over to us. "I'm next. Want to watch?"

Suzie and I bolt up and follow her to the fitting chairs. Alison's danced on pointe since she turned twelve, but by the glow in her eyes, I can tell this is special for her. Alison kicks off her sneakers, leans forward, and shoots a wide grin at me. Madame Babikov's bones creak and pop as she kneels next to Alison.

"Right foot first." Madame Babikov holds Alison's bare foot in her hand and studies it. "I have not seen feet like this in long time." Using an old yellow sewing tape, she measures every angle of Alison's foot. "Excellent." She nods to herself, removes a small notepad from her pocket, and jots down various numbers. After repeating the same procedure with Alison's left foot, Madame Babikov extends a hand to her. "Please be kind to help me stand."

"Of course." Alison takes her hand and gently pulls her to her feet.

After Madam Babikov rises, she straightens her long black dress and pats Alison's arm. "Thank you, dear. Now, I need moment to compute figures." She hobbles to a wooden podium-type desk and removes a scroll of parchment paper from a drawer. After rolling out the paper, she scribbles away, stopping only to wipe her glasses. While we wait, she continues unraveling more parchment and writing more equations. Every few minutes, she shakes her head and mumbles.

One of the teens crosses her arms. "None of us took that long," she mutters to the girl next to her.

"I hear what you tell her," Madame Babikov says. "Matters of the big importance cannot be rushed."

After scribbling one last set of numbers, Madame Babikov glances up, her hooded eyes glazed. "Solved. Miss Natalia, please be kind to climb ladder and retrieve shoebox number 398. Is on top shelf, row A."

"Of course." Miss Natalia swings the ladder around and climbs up.

Alison smiles, eager with anticipation.

"Found them," Miss Natalia calls out. "There's just one problem."

"Problem?" Madame Babikov says.

Alison's face drops.

We all crane our necks and see a black cat draped across the top of the box.

"Koshka," Madame Babikov shouts. "Off."

The cat yawns and stretches its long scraggly limbs.

"Now." Madame Babikov pounds her cane on the floor.

Koshka rises and slinks over to another box.

"Old cats." Madame Babikov shakes her head. "They sleep most of day, but still have the adventures at night. They know more than they say."

As Miss Natalia climbs down with the box, she says, "I never noticed before—Koshka has two different colored eyes."

Madame Babikov nods. "One amber and one indigo." Madame Babikov points to me. "Almost like you." She leans in closer and squints. "Except yours more like Prussian blue and gingerbread brown."

I glance up to look at the black cat's eyes, but he's no longer on the high shelf.

"Are these the right ones?" Miss Natalia asks, handing Madame Babikov the pink box.

Madame Babikov opens the lid and removes the pink satin pointe shoes from the tissue paper. "Yes, thank you, dear." She pulls a clump of lamb's wool from her pocket and forms it to Alison's toes. "Some dancers prefer use gel pads, or just the paper towels. But for my rubles, I like old fashion lamb's wool."

As everyone watches intently, she slips the shoes on Alison and tightens the drawstrings. "Arch right foot on floor," Madame Babikov says.

Alison places the tip of her toes on the floor and pushes her foot forward.

"Splendid. Now hold on me and stand on toes. Look in mirror."

Alison rises to full pointe. Her face glows as she stares at her reflection. "They feel great," she says.

"Perfection. Unimprovable. They help with the blisters, you see. You may take off now. I will darn ribbons later."

After Alison hands them back, I run over and hug her. "You're so lucky. I wish I could get pointe shoes today. I'll probably wait a million years before I get mine—if I ever get them."

"Hang in there. Don't think everything's so rosy at my age." Alison's glow fades and her blue eyes darken. Other thoughts have invaded her mind—most likely Dylan thoughts.

As Alison slips her sneakers back on, Suzie whispers to me, "Teens are so moody."

After two more students finish with their fittings, Miss Natalia gathers us around. "Dancers." She claps her hands. "We'll be leaving now. Please thank Madame Babikov."

"Thank you, Madame Babikov," the students singsong.

"My pleasure, children. I get working and sew ribbons on your pointe shoes now."

"I'll send Jeremiah back later to pick them up." Miss Natalia gives Madame Babikov a good-bye hug and kisses her on both cheeks.

I start toward the door when something rubs my ankle. It's the black cat.

Madame Babikov smiles. "Ah, Koshka like you."

I bend to pet him and we lock our mismatched eyes for a moment—almost as if he wants to tell me something important. Since I don't speak cat, I can only shrug.

After we all meander back up Praity Lane to Main Street, Miss Natalia surprises us with a stop at the ice cream parlor. I order a vanilla banana split with hot fudge melted on top. When we finish, we head to the rear parking lot. Jeremiah appears a few minutes later, and we climb into the purple bus.

When we arrive back at the school, some of the other students run out to the bus to greet us. They tell us Madame Dupree has just posted our classes on the bulletin board in the parlor. I hold my breath and rush inside with the other girls. During the stampede, I'm shoved to the back, and the taller girls in front of the board block my view. I stand on my toes but still can't see over their heads. Finally, they move out of the way.

CHAPTER
SEVEN

Oh No, Not the Pixie Ds!

On the placement list, I spot Alison's name first; she's in a group called Prima As. I'm sure that's the best class in her age division—she's always with the most advanced dancers. Below her group are Prima Bs, Cs, and Ds. I skip over the boy's section and see Suzie's name in a group called Pixie As. There are ten names in her group. I read them over again, searching for mine. My name is not there. I keep reading down the list. I go to Pixie Bs. Nope. Pixie Cs? Nada. My eyes scan all the way to the bottom of the board. My poor name, Kiki MacAdoo, is in the last group on the board for all to see. I'm assigned to the Pixie Ds.

Suzie lowers her eyes. "I wish we were together," she says.

I try to hold back my tears of disappointment. "Me too." I look around for Alison, but she's talking to one of the girls from her pointe class.

"We're in the same class," a voice says behind me.

I turn. It's the little popsicle-orange haired girl. The one who gets nauseated when she turns.

"I'm Darla," she says.

Something isn't right here. "How old are you, Darla?" I ask.

"Eight and a half." She smiles, revealing a wide gap where her front teeth should be.

I feel my face burn. Here I am, almost twelve, with the eight-year-olds. That's just peachy.

I rush over to Alison and tug her arm. "I have to talk to you," I say.

She takes a few steps away from the other girls. "What's up?"

"Did you see where they put me?" I whisper.

She pushes a hair back from her face. "Sorry, I didn't notice."

My chin trembles. "Pixie Ds—the absolute worst group. You can't get any worse."

"Don't get so upset. Just do the best you can."

"I want to go home," I say, trying hard not to cry in front of everybody.

"You know you can't. Dad's not coming back for three weeks."

"I wish Mom were still alive, so I could go home." The words are out before I can stop them.

Alison hugs me, and I can tell I've made her a little sad. "I wish she were too, Squeak."

I hardly eat anything during dinner and toss all night. When I wake up, I give myself a little pep talk to try to make the best of it. During breakfast, I manage to eat some cereal, but when the bell rings for classes to begin, my stomach knots.

Suzie grins and says she'll see me at lunch. I force a smile and watch her head to the Pixie As' studio. Another girl from Suzie's class catches up with her, and the two of them giggle as they enter their dance room.

While I stand frozen, I hear a lispy voice say, "Hurry up, or we'll be late."

It's Darla again, her freckled face smiling at me. I walk with her down the long hall to the Pixie Ds' dance room. When I peek inside to see what I'm facing, it's just what I feared—a group of girls from eight and up. I bet I'm the oldest in this class. I swallow hard and hesitate at the doorway.

"Come on," Darla says, her face beaming. "You can stand by me." She grabs my hand and pulls me in the room.

I try to shake her hand loose, but she has a tight little grip. "Don't be shy," she says. Which makes the whole situation a billion times worse. The other girls all stare at me and whisper to one another. I catch my reflection in the mirror—a pathetic eleven-and-a-half-year-old being dragged in by a tiny eight-year-old.

Miss Genevieve is waiting by the stereo, counting heads. "Good, all twelve of you are here. We shall begin."

She starts us at the barre and demonstrates a series of exercises. After that, we move across the floor and do center work. At least I'm short for my age, so I'm not the tallest girl in class. But still, the whole experience is super degrading. I can't imagine three weeks of this. Some of these squirts are better than I am. Two of the eight-year-olds are like little tops when they turn, and a couple have *arabesques* that rise to the height of their shoulders. I can't even manage a ninety degree one.

The two-hour class goes on for a lifetime. I scan the room for a clock but can't find one. When the class finally ends, Miss Genevieve reminds us that we have an hour break before lunch. I shake little Darla loose and run out to the parlor to find Alison or Suzie. The parlor is empty, so I try the garden. Alison's not out there, but Suzie is. She's jumping double Dutch rope with the Pixie A girls. She catches my eye and waves at me to come over. I consider it, but I stink so bad at double Dutch, I can't get even get inside the two swinging ropes without tripping.

I've had enough humiliation for one day, so I run up to my room and pass the time alone drawing ballerinas in my favorite poses. Before I know it, the lunch bell rings, and it's time to face everyone again.

As soon as I enter the dining hall, I search for Alison. I overhear someone say her group, the Prima As, have an extra class today and are scheduled for lunch an hour later. So much for sitting with my sister. I scan the room for Suzie and see her enter with the Pixie As. She smiles and motions for me to join her group. I take a breath and head over.

By the time I get to Suzie, I wind up sitting three girls away from her. The girls on each side of me talk about dance combinations they worked on during class. I try to think of something interesting or funny to say, but my head is like a cartoon with an empty thought bubble.

After lunch, I have two more classes with the Pixie Ds: one lyrical and one jazz. The jazz class is fun, but even in that class, I'm in the back line—the place teachers put girls who mess up the steps. No matter how hard I try, I can't concentrate on all those contractions, triplets, and calypso turns. The part of me that wants to give up and go home grows bigger.

After class, I climb the three flights to my room again. Suzie's still not there. It's lonely by myself, but I can't face all those other girls. Mom used to say that fresh air helps when you feel down, so I stuff my sketchbooks and colored pencils into my backpack. With an hour and a half before dinner, I head outside to search for something to draw.

Out back, some girls are dancing in the open air and others are doing cartwheels. I hurry past them, following the path to the theater. Beyond it to the right, I find an arched white gate entwined with red roses. The gate is unlocked but creaks when I swing it open. I glance behind me. Nobody is there to tell me not to go, so I step under the arch and shut the gate behind me. In front of me lies a winding stone path. I follow the path as it meanders through giant hedges arranged in a maze.

A sparrow shoots out from the hedge and grazes past my glasses. "Hey, be careful," I mutter.

The path turns at sharp angles. At one juncture, I come upon an iron bench with a furry black squirrel perched on it. I wonder if it's good or bad luck. I've never seen a black squirrel before—only grey ones. When I reach into my bag for my sketchpad, the squirrel scurries away. How can I draw these animals if they won't sit still?

I wind through the hedges until I come upon an open meadow sprinkled with blue and pink wildflowers. In the center of the field, a dark-haired boy is running, waving a stick that makes giant, multi-colored bubbles. It's the shy boy from the dining hall. He's headed toward me at first, but then veers and disappears into the woods on the other side. He must not have seen me.

"Hey! Wait for me," I yell, and run across the meadow to catch up with him.

CHAPTER EIGHT

A Fuzzy Thief

By the time I reach the far end of the pasture, I'm out of breath. About where the boy disappeared into the woods, I find a twisted dirt path, and after I rest a moment, I follow it between the rows of massive trees. A thick canopy of leaves and pines darken the sky. I call out to the boy again, but all I hear are hundreds of birds chattering away. They sure have lots to talk about today. Maybe they're discussing which branches are the most excellent ones to build nests. Or maybe they're talking about me.

"I'm not that fascinating," I tell the birds.

But maybe all that chattering is some kind of warning. My steps slow and then I stop, wondering if I'm allowed to go past this point. There's no sign that says *Do Not Enter*. And that boy is in here somewhere. Madame Dupree said not to go deep into the forest and not to cross some lake. This is only the beginning of the forest, so I guess it's fine.

As I start walking again, my foot steps on something squishy. I glance down. It seems I've squashed a purple mushroom that's part of a circle.

"Mind where you step," a high-pitched voice squeals behind me.

Startled, I spin around to see… a bush. I must be hearing things. I shrug it off and continue my search for the dark-haired boy. Thorny branches reach over the narrow path and scrape my legs, but I push through and keep going.

Up ahead, one of the boy's bubbles floats in an open clearing. It bobs down the path away from me, and I follow it until it bursts—right at the edge of a lake. I bite my lip and pause. This must be the lake Madame Dupree warned us about—the one we're never to cross. But whose red rowboat is that docked on the other side? Did that boy row it over there? There's another brown boat on this side, but I'm not climbing in and rowing after him. No way. Maybe he doesn't care about breaking rules, but I'm in no mood to get in trouble today.

I pull out my sketchpad and search for something to draw. That's what I came here to do anyway. By the shoreline, a group of wildflowers catches my attention. I sit on a nearby tree stump and take out my tin case filled with colored pencils. As I study the shapes and shading of the petals, a floral scent fills the air. One of the violet flowers stands out from the rest. The velvet petals resemble the tutus from the *Dance of the Flowers.*

As I study the flower, I realize there's a tiny heart-shaped face in the center of the flower studying me. It stares at me with sparkling jade-green eyes, almost too small to make out. I gasp and drop all my pencils. My insides tingle and buzz, and my hand flies up to my face. Yep, I've definitely got my glasses on. But how could such a tiny person live in a flower? How could there even be such a tiny person? First the brochure, then the floating blue lights—and now this?

"Hello?" I ask shakily, unsure of what else to do.

The eyes blink at me. When I blink back, the tiny creature is gone. I'm still in shock, but I know I didn't imagine it. I glare at the wildflower, hoping the face will pop out again. But it doesn't.

I grab my pencils and start sketching the flower and the face I saw, trying to get myself to believe I just saw a... a *fairy*. I never want to forget what it looked like.

I'm unsure how much time passes while I sit there drawing. Alison says I get lost in my own world whenever I sketch. I have to erase the flower portrait countless times before I am halfway pleased—I've never had to capture such dainty features before! Luckily, I don't gouge a hole in the paper.

As I stand to stretch out the kinks in my body, I return my attention to the real world. From the chill in the air and the fading blue sky, I realize it must be late. I hope I'm not in trouble.

While I hurry and gather my art supplies, the smell of a burning fireplace fills the air. Someone must live out here in the forest. Maybe it's Jeremiah. He did say his cabin was in the woods. But what if it's someone else? Maybe this is someone else's land and they don't like random little girls in their front yard, no matter how big it is.

As I rush to find the pathway back, my foot catches on a large stone and my whole body flies forward. I catch myself, but my glasses fly off and crack against another rock. I pick them up carefully. Both lenses are scratched and the frame is so mangled, I can't even wear them.

"You idiot," I scold myself. I'm lucky I didn't break my nose, but without my glasses, everything is just a big blur. But I have to get back to the school before dark. I hold my twisted glasses carefully, trying not to damage them any more than they already are.

"Don't panic," I keep repeating. All I have to do is re-trace my steps.

The woods are silent now as I head toward the haze of trees. It's like one of those nightmares where you can't find your way home, but this is real. It's bad enough I can't see where I'm going, but now I sense something stalking me. As I run forward, twigs crack behind me.

I jump and drop my glasses. "Not again," I groan. But at this point, does it even matter? "Go away!" I yell to whoever is behind me.

When I turn, all I see is a fuzzy black shape staring at me. "Oh, it's you," I say to the black squirrel. As I bend to pick up my glasses, the squirrel grabs them. He examines them with his tiny hand-paws.

"Drop them," I command, pointing to the ground for emphasis.

The black squirrel freezes. But as I reach out for my glasses, the squirrel scampers into the woods, still clutching them.

"Bring them back!" I scream.

I can't tell for sure—my eyesight is significantly impaired, after all—but it looks like he turned and sneered at me. I chase after him and yell until my voice goes hoarse, but it's no use. The squirrel is nowhere in sight. I'm near the lake again, and I hear rippling. I head closer and peek out from behind a bush.

It's someone on a rowboat. They're rowing to my side of the shore.

"Wait up," a boy's voice shouts from the boat.

I can't make out his features, but he has dark hair. He must be the same boy from before. I pause a moment. Can I trust him? He *is* coming from the off-limits side of the lake. But if he is the same boy, he's a student at the conservatory like me and could lead me back. I don't have much choice at this point. The sky is violet now, and if I get lost, I'll wind up spending the whole night in the dark woods. I decide to wait for him.

A few minutes later, he drags his boat onto my side of the shore. "If we hurry," he says in a raspy voice, "we can get back before dark." He tucks his oars inside the boat. "They won't even know you were gone. Follow me." He coughs into his elbow and then motions for me to follow.

I remain in my spot. "Sorry, but I don't know you. How do I know that you're taking me back to the conservatory? Plus," I take a step away from him, "you sound sick. I don't want to catch anything."

"A, I'm not sick. This is how my voice always sounds. And B, you know me. I saw you looking at me in the dining hall."

I squint at him, but it's no use. "I can't see too well. A squirrel stole my glasses."

"Which one?"

"I only have one pair of glasses—my purple ones. I told my father that he should buy—"

"I meant which squirrel?"

"Oh. It was all black."

"That's Ziggy. I'll talk to him tomorrow. We've got to go now before you get in trouble." He begins to run up the path.

I follow, stumbling a little. "Wait, squirrels listen to you?"

"Sometimes," he says.

"You're a student at Mount Faylinn—right?"

"Yeah. I already told you I saw you before."

"You could be lying."

"Watch this," he says. He runs three steps and *grand jeté* leaps between two pine trees. "And now this." He runs again, but this time he adds a perfect switch leap, changing legs midair from a right split to a left split.

"Showoff," I mutter under my breath.

"Hurry up. They're serving spaghetti with meatballs tonight."

By the time we reach the conservatory, the sky is black. We rush to the dining hall, but it's empty. The clock on the wall says eight thirty.

"Uh-oh. We missed dinner," I say. "They must know we wandered off."

He points behind me and I look over my shoulder to see Madame Dupree entering the room. Her shoes click the floor as she heads toward us.

"Don't worry, I'll cover for you," he whispers. "What's your name by the way? I'm Oliver."

"Kiki," I say in a hushed tone. "But who's going to cover for you?"

He flashes an impish grin. "I can go wherever I please, whenever I please."

Madame Dupree crosses her arms and tilts her head. "Where were you, young lady?"

My empty stomach twists. "I went out to sketch and I—"

"I invited Kiki to my place to show her some comic books." Oliver turns to me. "Right?"

I lower my eyes. "I—"

Madam Dupree sighs. "Next time, Oliver, make sure she's back before dinner. I don't want any of the girls wandering out there in the dark. And, Kiki—"

I dutifully look up. "Yes, Madame Dupree?"

"You're to follow the rules from now on. Understand?"

I nod solemnly.

"Good." Madame Dupree turns and starts walking away.

I stand there a moment hoping to talk to Oliver alone, but Madame Dupree glances back and claps her hands. "Off to your rooms. Now."

As soon as she turns again, Oliver's eyes catch mine. He flashes me a quick grin before we head our separate ways. When I get up to my room, Suzie is holding a hairbrush like a microphone and singing along to a pop song. As soon as she notices me, she smiles and lowers the music.

"I didn't see you in the dining hall," she says. "I figured you ate later with your sister." She stares at me a moment. "Hey, where are your glasses?"

When I tell her a black squirrel stole them, I wait for her mouth to drop open.

Instead, she nods. "My labradoodle is a sneaky thief too," she says, giggling. "He loves to steal socks from the laundry basket. Then he hides them all under my bed."

After we have a good laugh over that, I ask her not to tell Alison I went into the woods. "I don't need a scolding from her," I say.

Suzie seals her lips with an imaginary lock and key.

CHAPTER NINE

A Long Line of Crumbs

The next day, I sit with Suzie and her Pixie As' group during breakfast. Alison's class is on a different schedule again. I scan my eyes around the room, searching for Oliver. I have so many questions, but I can't see if he's anywhere in the dining hall. No matter how much I squint, everyone's face in the distance is a blur. I'll have to tell Madame Dupree about my glasses problem when I get the nerve. Oliver said he'd try to get them back from that squirrel, but even if he can, they're all mangled anyway.

I ask Suzie if Oliver's here. She glances around and says he's with the other boys in his usual spot—the far end of the long table next to mine. The thought of strolling over there with everyone staring at me makes my chest tighten, so I decide to wait until breakfast ends. In the meantime, I wolf down my scrambled eggs and bacon. I'm super hungry from missing dinner yesterday.

A half hour later when the bell rings, I jump up. While everyone crowds toward the doors, I hurry to Oliver's seat. By the time I get to the other end of the dining hall, he's gone.

During my morning dance classes, Darla glues herself to me once again. To make matters worse, she manages to squeak out a decent double *pirouette*. How humiliating. In my defense, it's hard to see the new steps Miss Genevieve is demonstrating without my glasses. But even if I could, I'm not concentrating on dance today. I'm waiting for the next chance to talk to Oliver alone.

During a break between lyrical class and lunch, I get lucky. I catch him heading down the hall, and he's by himself. I give him a quick wave.

"Hey," he says.

"You have a minute? I wanted to ask you—"

One of the other boys comes up from behind. He gives me a funny look and pushes Oliver forward.

"Come on, dude," he says to Oliver. "We gotta go."

"Go ahead," Oliver tells him. "I'll catch up." Oliver then turns to me and whispers, "Meet me at four in the theater."

When four o'clock comes around, I rush outside and follow the stone path to the theater building. The air is sticky from the late afternoon sun. As soon as I open the heavy blue theater door and enter the lobby, the air turns cool and dark. The lights aren't on, and I pause, waiting for my eyes to adjust.

"Oliver?" I shout, staring into the blackness. Soon I can make out hazy shapes and a faint glow, like a nightlight, somewhere backstage. After groping my way through an open door into the auditorium, I yell for Oliver again.

I have no idea where the light switches are, and the theater remains silent, so I sit on a velvet seat in the back row and wait. It's too quiet here—so quiet, I can hear my own breathing. Way too creepy for me to stay alone. I decide to count down from twenty-five. If he's not here by then, I'll leave.

Twenty-five, twenty-four, twenty-three, twenty—

Something moves on the stage. A dancer, I think, wearing a white, wispy costume, turning in a circle. Maybe they're rehearsing.

"Hi," I yell out.

The dancer stops and then vanishes. She must have just run off stage, but it looked like she disappeared into thin air. An icy breeze brushes past me and my skin tingles. Forget counting down—I'm out of here. I rush to the front door and push it.

The heavy door won't budge. It's either stuck or locked. "Come on, open," I mutter. I give the door another hard push. No luck. As I step back to try with a running start, a hand touches my shoulder. I freeze.

"You leaving?" a scratchy voice asks.

I swing around. It's too dark to make out who's behind me.

"It's me, Oliver." He flicks on the lobby lights. "See?"

I touch my pounding heart. "Don't scare me like that."

"I'm sorry, I—"

"Wait," I say. "How the heck did you get in here?"

"The backdoor stage entrance."

"Then you saw that dancer onstage. Who was she?"

Oliver glances around. "What dancer?"

"She was there a second ago, wearing a white costume."

"We're the only two people here. You don't see that great without your glasses, do you? Come on, we're going to the woods now to get them back." Oliver opens the front blue door with one shove.

The sun is blinding, and I shield my eyes with my hand. When I can see again, Oliver is staring at me.

"Hey, I just noticed," he says. "You're so lucky."

"Me? I'm not lucky about anything."

"You have ghost eyes."

"I have what?"

"Ghost eyes. My grandad says a person born with two different colored eyes can see the earthly realm and the ghostly realm at the same time."

"I've never heard that."

"It's an excellent talent—very useful around these parts."

I want to ask him what he means by that, but the back door of the conservatory bursts open and students pour out. I hear the boys' voices among them, yelling and laughing.

"Follow me," Oliver says, taking a path I hadn't seen that leads out of sight of the garden. "I don't want the guys seeing me. They don't know about the secrets of the forest. If I told them, they'd only make fun of me."

Secrets?

"First I have to get something," he says.

I follow him to a side door into the conservatory. It leads straight into the kitchen. Inside, Louise is sitting at a table eating a slice of peach pie. The warm sweet aroma swirls through the room.

"Oops," she says, glancing up. "You caught me. I just baked them and couldn't resist. But don't worry—there's plenty for everyone." She points to a rack of pies cooling. "You'll all get a slice for dessert tonight."

"Can't wait," Oliver says. "Right now, though, I have a taste for an apple and some nuts. Is it okay if I get some?"

"Help yourself. I won't tell if you don't." Louise winks.

Oliver collects his snack items and places them in a plastic bag. "Thanks," he says and motions for me to follow him out.

Once outside, he glances around. All the children's voices are coming from the play areas out back.

"This way." Oliver clutches the plastic bag and runs past the kitchen dumpsters. Beyond the garden shed, he crouches between two pine trees. "I don't want the other kids to see where we're going."

"What about your snack?" I ask. "Aren't you going to eat it?"

He smiles, then turns to push deeper into the forest between the pines. "It's not for me, it's for Ziggy. We have to find him before it gets dark. Hurry, follow me—army style."

I crouch along with Oliver under the dense trees, crawling and stepping on cushions of brown needles. Even though it's the middle of summer, the crisp pine scent reminds me of December. I picture the perfect present waiting for me under the Christmas tree—pink pointe shoes.

"What do you want for the holidays?" I ask, pushing a branch from my eyes.

"The holidays?" Oliver says, amused. "You're thinking about presents already?"

I inhale deeply through my nose. "It smells so Christmassy here."

"That pine smell is one of the things I love about living in the forest."

"You live here?"

"Yep," he says, swatting a fly from his face.

"At the conservatory?" I ask.

"We have a cabin in the woods."

I get a slight shiver. "What side of the lake?"

"This side, of course."

"Do you live near Jeremiah? He told me he lives in the woods."

"I live with Jeremiah. He's my grandfather."

"Oh." I let that sink in. "So your full name is Oliver Crumb?"

He nods. "I come from a long line of Crumbs. But I'm the last of them."

I can't help but giggle. He turns and shoots me a look.

"Sorry, I pictured a trail of breadcrumbs across a kitchen floor."

"Yeah, I get that a lot."

I feel like I've hurt his feelings, so I try to make him feel better. "Everyone makes fun of my name too. It's no big deal."

"I guess." He shrugs.

"So, do your parents live in the cabin too?" I ask.

His mouth tightens—the way mine does when I don't want to cry. "It's just my grandfather and me," he says.

I don't press. I know the feeling when part of you is missing.

We continue crawling under the pines until a path opens up. I'm relieved when we're finally able to stand and stretch our legs.

Oliver sticks out his arms and studies them. "Check yourself for ticks."

I give my legs and arms the once over. "All clear—except for this little guy." I brush off a beetle. "I bet it's neat having a cabin in the forest. You must really know your way around here."

"The way most girls know their way around the mall." He smirks.

"Hey, boys have to shop for clothes too."

"Yeah, but with us, it's get in and out of the store—as fast as we can."

"Talking about stores—do you have an optometrist in town?"

He lifts his chin and gives me a smug smile. "I have perfect vision—actually better than perfect."

"Of course you do," I say. "Just like your perfect leaps. But how am I supposed to get glasses?"

"Grandad goes to a place off Main Street. But I heard the doctor's on vacation now. If we get your old ones back from Ziggy, I know someone who might fix them."

"Your grandad?"

"No, he's great with carpentry and plumbing and stuff, but Mr. Orenpuck's the expert for smaller things."

"That would be great. It's hard when life's fuzzy."

"First we have to find Ziggy. He's a bad-mannered squirrel, but he goes crazy over apples and nuts. I know most of his routes and favorite trees, but we have to hurry. He can cover a lot of ground."

I chase Oliver around the forest, searching one tree after another. After a half hour, Oliver points, and I see a black blur scamper up a locust tree.

"Ziggy," Oliver shouts, running to the base of the tree.

The squirrel ignores him and continues climbing higher.

Oliver opens the plastic bag and holds it up. "We've got your favorites."

Ziggy glances down.

"A delicious apple and a bunch of crunchy nuts—all for you."

The squirrel leaps from his high branch to a lower one and scurries down the trunk. He stands on his back legs and reaches out with his tiny claw-paws.

"Not so fast." Oliver yanks back the bag. "These are for you on one condition."

Ziggy tilts his head.

"Hand over Kiki's glasses."

Ziggy scampers away a few feet, pauses, and glances back. Then he goes a few feet farther and looks at us again

"He wants us to follow him. Let's go."

The squirrel hurries deeper into the forest, zigzagging through massive pines and prickly bramble. While I rush to keep up, thorns scrape my arms and legs. Eventually, we come upon a winding trail of pebbles lined with bluebells. It leads to a narrow stream tinkling over odd-shaped stones. The stones look like someone carved faces into them—like a mini Mount Rushmore. But since I don't have my glasses, I'm probably completely wrong.

Ziggy pauses a moment and looks back, checking if we're still behind him. He then scurries underneath the drooping branches of a willow tree by the water's edge. I duck under and pause, squinting while I catch my breath. It looks like Ziggy is surrounded by tiny dollhouse furniture with everything set up like a patio on the mossy ground. I lean in for a closer look. Miniature chairs made from twigs and vines are arranged in a circle. Within the circle, red dotted mushroom stools line a glass counter.

"It figures," Oliver says.

"What?"

"There they are. Can't you see them?"

"What are you talking about? I see twig chairs, mushrooms, and a counter made of two glass circles."

"Those are your glasses. See the purple rims? They dug the stems into the ground so they stand up like that. It looks like Mr. Orenpuck already unmangled them."

I narrow my eyes and realize those *are* my glasses-turned-countertop. "Who did all this?" I ask, shocked.

"The wee folk, of course."

CHAPTER TEN

A Lesson Learned

"What on earth are *wee folk*?"

"Fairies," Oliver says, without a hint of sarcasm. "But if you talk to them, call them the good folk—or by their Gaelic name. You pronounce it *shee*, but it's spelled s-i-d-h-e."

"Wait a minute." Images of the lights outside Alison's window and the face in the flower race through my head, but I try to focus on what Oliver is saying. "I've seen that strange word somewhere." I rack my brain trying to remember. "How is it spelled again?"

Oliver raises his index finger and writes the letters in the air.

My whole body tingles. "That's the word my brochure spelled out in gold letters—right in my kitchen."

"Cool" is all Oliver says. He's a little too calm—anyone else wouldn't have believed me. But Oliver isn't like anyone else I've met.

"So… you really do have fairies here?"

Oliver nods. "The woods are filled with them," he pauses, his face suddenly serious, "along with much scarier things."

I gulp and scan the surrounding forest with my blurry eyes. "Yesterday, I saw a violet flower that had a face."

His expression lightens. "Those are just the flower fairies."

I grin and clasp my hands. "I knew it."

"We have all kinds around here." He says it like it's the most normal thing in the world.

I shake my head as I crouch closer to my glasses. I've had enough blurriness. When I squint, I see that two tiny teacups are set on my eyeglass-table. "What nerve." As I carefully remove the cups, Ziggy rises on his hind legs and cries out with loud clicks. His black hairy tail jerks and kinks as he bares his teeth at me.

"Wait," Oliver shouts, although I already froze when Ziggy started chittering. "Don't touch your glasses yet. Ziggy might bite you." Oliver tosses the apple and nuts to him.

Ziggy grabs the apple, and while he nibbles it with supersonic speed, I dig around the moss to free the stems of my glasses. I work carefully, so I don't twist them. After I release them, I puff breath on the lenses and buff them with my t-shirt. When I put them on, they fit perfectly. There's not a scratch on them.

After I duck out from under the willow tree, I peer at the forest near and far. Everything is nice and sharp. "Hallelujah," I say. "Now that I've got my glasses, can you lead me back? It's getting dark and I can't be late again."

Oliver's eyebrows slant with disapproval. "You can't take them without leaving something in return."

"Leave something?" The sharp tone of my voice surprises me, but nothing Oliver says makes sense. "They're my glasses. I have every right to take them."

Oliver peers around, a worried expression creasing his forehead. "Don't you have anything to give the fairies?"

I sigh and check my pockets. "No, and even if I did, why should I? They stole them."

"Technically, Ziggy stole them, and Mr. Orenpuck fixed them."

"Who is he anyway?" I demand.

"One of the fairy elders." Again, Oliver acts like this stuff is common knowledge.

"He only fixed them for his own selfish purpose—to use them in his house, or whatever you call that outdoor living room. I've got to go, and I'm leaving with my glasses." I stomp away.

"Suit yourself. But don't say I didn't warn you. You're in for a heap of bad luck now," Oliver says grimly.

I ignore him and continue on my way.

"Hey," he yells. "You're heading in the wrong direction." He catches up with me. "I'll lead you halfway back until you know where you are."

After Oliver guides me to the path I'm familiar with, he heads off in another direction—to his grandad's cabin, I guess, but I don't really care. As I continue on, I come upon a trail of shiny looking pebbles. After a closer inspection, I see that they're all silver dollars. *Sweet!* Since they're on the path I'm headed, I pick them up as I move along. Every silver dollar is heads up.

"*Bad luck?* You're so wrong, Oliver," I say to myself as I fill my pockets.

Soon the coins veer off my path, leading to an old oak tree about twenty feet away. Since the tree is so close, I head toward it and continue collecting the silver dollars. Maybe the next time we're in town I can buy a cool gift for Alison's birthday.

After I pick up the last silver dollar at the base of the tree's trunk, something sparkles within a knotted hollow. I peer in for a closer look and gasp. Deep within are stacks of more silver coins. One voice in my head says I shouldn't take any of them—they're not mine. But another voice says, "Someone led you here. They must want you to have them." I stick my hand inside the tree hollow. I grab a handful of coins, but before I pull them out, something stings my thumb.

"Ow," I yell as I yank out my hand. While I examine my swelling finger, I hear a buzzing sound. It starts soft, almost distant, but soon, it's deafening. I know that sound. I scream and run back to the path as fast as I can. A second later, hundreds of wasps fly out of the tree hollow. They swirl into a black blur and chase me.

"Help!" I scream. I run like a bullet back to school, swatting as some wasps catch up to me. When I reach the gardens, the students stare at me, pausing in their games.

"Wasps," I shriek.

All the children scream and run inside with me. We slam the door shut and peek through the window. Outside, Jeremiah grabs a hose and sprays the angry swarm. He keeps them at bay until they finally retreat. As I watch him, my thumb starts to throb. It's grown twice its normal size. Then my legs start burning. I glance down and count nine red welts on my legs and arms.

Suzie rushes through the crowd and cries out when she sees the stings. "Oh Kiki! Those look awful!"

I try not to cry.

Jeremiah pushes through the door and addresses us. "They're all gone. Did anyone get stung?"

"Kiki did," Suzie says.

He hurries over. "Are you allergic?"

"No," I say, still holding back the tears.

"Good. Since they were wasps, not bees, you won't have any stingers in you. But it's still going to hurt. Come with me to the kitchen so we can fix you up."

"I'll go with you," Suzie says.

When we get to the kitchen, Louise is there, munching on potato chips. She glances up. "Everything all right?"

"Kiki had a bout of bad luck today." Jeremiah turns to me and raises his eyebrows. "Isn't that right?"

I feel like he can read my thoughts. Maybe he does have a touch of scary to him. I lower my head. "Yes. But I won't do anything like that again."

"You must be very careful around these woods." He then turns to Louise. "Can you wash her stings while I prepare the paste?"

"What are you going to do to her?" Suzie asks, eyes wide.

Louise laughs. "Don't worry, dear. After I wash Kiki's bites, I'll apply baking soda paste to reduce the swelling and help with the itching. Then I'll add honey to kill any bacteria, along with some garlic and lavender oil for good measure. They're great for treating any inflammation. Kiki will be as good as gold."

At the mention of the word *gold*, I suddenly feel the weight of all those silver coins in my pockets and get a nervous twinge in my stomach.

"Sounds like a witch's brew," Suzie says skeptically.

"You'll be surprised how well it works," Jeremiah says as he gathers the ingredients.

After they finish treating me, I thank them both and head out to the parlor with Suzie. Alison is sitting on the velvet sofa with a couple of girls from her class. When she sees me, she jumps up and gives me a hug. I let out a little yelp.

"What's wrong?" She backs away a step and looks me up and down. "What are those white spots?"

"Kiki got a million wasp bites," Suzie says, grimacing. "That's the baking soda paste to make them heal."

Alison winces. "Oh no. How did that happen?"

"I was somewhere I shouldn't have been, doing something I shouldn't have. And it's only nine bites on my legs and arms and one on my thumb—not a million."

"Be more careful next time, Squeak."

"I just noticed," Suzie says, staring at my face. "You got your glasses back. Did that squirrel from the woods return them?"

I shoot her a warning *be quiet* look.

Alison narrows her eyes at me. "When did you lose your glasses?"

"Yesterday. I kind of misplaced them." I shrug.

"And what's this about a squirrel?"

"I was only joking," Suzie says. She slips a hand behind her back where I can see and crosses her fingers.

Bing, bong, bing, the loudspeaker rings, interrupting us. Madame Dupree's announcement reminds us that since today is Friday, we may pick up our cell phones from the dining room. Alison gives me one more serious look, tells me again to be careful, then joins the stampede of everyone who has a phone—which is everyone except me and the younger kids. They all point and stare at my white wasp bites. How humiliating. I'm not only phoneless but foolish. It was pretty dumb of me to fall for that fairy trick.

CHAPTER ELEVEN

A Bad Idea?

After we all head to the dining hall, Alison, Suzie, and I sit together. During dinner, Alison hardly eats anything and remains quiet. I thought she'd grill me more about my glasses, but instead, she stares off into space and picks at her blue nail polish.

I'm almost afraid to ask, but I have to. "Is everything okay?" I take a quick breath. "It's not Dad, is it?"

Alison shakes her head.

"Did you hear from him?"

"He has no cell reception on the dig, remember? But I'm sure he's fine."

So it's Dylan trouble. I hate talking about him, so instead I say, "How's Mila's broken leg? Did she text you?"

"Yes." Alison's eyes remain distant.

"Uh-oh. Does she have to get an operation? When one of the kids from school broke his elbow, the doctor drilled screws into his bones. Then the screws started poking out, and he had to have two more operations."

Suzie's mouth falls open. "Eww—gross. Does your friend Mila need screws like that?"

Alison shakes her head. "Turns out she didn't break her leg. It was only a sprain. She doesn't even need crutches now—just an ace bandage."

"That's a relief," I say. "Is she coming to the conservatory late?"

"The doctor told her to wait to do any dance until September."

I take a bite of my peach pie. "That must be a bummer for her."

"I guess." Alison pushes away her untouched plate. "Mila said she'll try to make the best of summer. She's been hanging out with Dylan and the gang. Apparently, he had a big pool party yesterday."

Not good. Not good. My radar's going off. I know Alison wishes she could have gone to that party.

"I miss swimming in my pool," Suzie says. "But my parents said sometimes I'll have to give up fun things if I want to improve at dance. It's all worth it in the end." Suzie peers at Alison. "Right?"

Alison glances down at her phone and remains silent.

After dinner, Suzie and I make our way to the rec room. Alison says she's tired and goes upstairs to her own room. Suzie and I play a few games of pinball and then head over to the nok hockey board. While we're whacking at the puck, Madame Dupree enters the room. Looking a bit ghoulish wrapped in her shawl and black scarves, she heads straight to me. Her powdery-rose perfume surrounds me, and I swallow hard. All the girls stop what they're doing and stare. I hope I'm not in trouble.

With her angled body looming over me, she narrows her eyes. "Kiara?"

"No," I say, relieved. "I'm Kiki."

"That's what I meant. Please come with me."

I shoot a quick glance at Suzie, who bites her lip. I follow Madame Dupree down the long hall of dioramas and enter what must be her office. Inside, crooked black-and-white photos of ballet dancers cover the walls. I wonder if any of them are of her—she's so old now, I can't tell. She removes a pile of books from a dainty embroidered chair and motions for me to sit. A long moment passes while she glares at a giant appointment calendar on her desk.

I shift from one position to another, waiting for her to yell at me for going into the forest. After a minute or two, I can't take the silence any longer. "I didn't cross the lake."

She glances up. "Sorry dear, did you say something about a rake? Back in my day, our stages were all raked. They made turns on pointe quite difficult."

I rub my head and stare at her.

"You don't know what that means, do you? Stages were tilted to help the audience see all of the performers. Many in Europe still are—including my beloved Paris Opera House. That is why we use the terms 'upstage' and 'downstage.' Upstage was the higher, rear part of the stage, and downstage was the lower part nearer the audience. Do you understand now?"

I always did get those two mixed up because they seemed backwards. But now it makes sense. "Yes, thank you," I say—even though I didn't ask.

"Good." She flips one of her scarves over her shoulder. "Is that what you came here to ask?"

Now I'm stumped. Do I lie and say yes? Or do I tell her I went out into the woods?

"Wait." Madame Dupree scratches her temple. "I think I called you in here. But I've completely forgotten why. Give me a moment." She lowers her head and stares at her calendar again. "I think it had something to do with dates."

She taps her pink pen with the pouf on top. "Ah, yes. I remember now—it's your sister."

"Alison?" Uh-oh, I hope she's not in trouble. But she never gets into trouble.

"I see on my calendar that your sister and another student have birthdays during camp. The girl turning nine lives nearby and her parents are picking her up for the day." Madame Dupree taps the calendar again and raises her chin. "What about Alison?"

"She's turning sixteen in two weeks," I say.

Madame Dupree nods. "Yes, I know. Does your family have any special plans for her?"

"It's just my dad and me, but he's digging up fossils in Australia. We're going to celebrate when he comes back."

"Oh my… Sixteen is an important milestone. My parents planned a big celebration for me when I turned that age."

"Was it fun?" I ask.

A shadow crosses her face. "My father died of a heart attack the night before. Instead of my party, we all attended his funeral. But we can't let her special day pass like any ordinary day. No, that just won't do." Madame Dupree's face lights up. "Why don't we throw her a surprise party? We can have it in the old ballroom. Hazel can bake a cake with vanilla and chocolate mousse, and I'll make crème brûlée. What do you think?"

Big parties make me nervous. They always feel like forced fun. You can't get caught standing alone if you don't want to look like a big loser. All that fun requires too much effort. But I don't want to tell her that.

"Well?"

I hesitate a moment longer. Alison would probably love having a big sweet sixteen party. And I do love chocolate mousse. I shrug. "Okay, I guess."

"Wonderful. But we mustn't let on it's for Alison's birthday—loose lips sink ships and all that. I'll tell the students we're having an open house and that they can invite two guests. You can invite Alison's friends ahead of time."

I immediately think of Mila and Dylan. I'd rather not talk to him, but it would cheer Alison up if he came. Maybe cheer her up is the wrong way to put it. I think Dylan makes her miserable whether he's around or not, but it's like she's addicted to him.

"Well?" Madame Dupree says. "Have you decided whom to invite?"

"One of her friends is a boy. Is that okay?"

"Yes, of course. Make sure her guests arrive before eight p.m. so we can hide them and their presents."

"But won't Alison call her friends herself to invite them?"

"Tell them to make up an excuse and say they can't come."

This all seems quite complicated, but it's better than Madame Dupree yelling at me for going into the woods.

Madame Dupree rises and leads me to the door. "So, we're all set? You'll make the calls?"

"I don't have a phone or their numbers." Part of me hopes that little snag puts an end to all this and I won't have to deal with Dylan or Mila.

"Let me think." Madame Dupree paces the small office.

I stand by the door waiting, staring at a board of keys hanging on the nearby wall. Arranged by floors, there must be well over a hundred, each with an attached tag with the room they unlock printed in neat block letters. After a few minutes I grow bored waiting, so I start jingling them.

"I have a duplicate set of every key in my two bottom desk drawers," she suddenly says.

I stop jingling. "What?"

"In case we lose any." She glances at me, her eyes confused. "Did you need a new key?"

I shake my head. *Aye yai yai*, as my grandmother used to say. Maybe she has short-term memory problems and this whole party idea has flown out of her head like a bird.

"No, I don't need anything." I turn the doorknob. "I was just leaving,"

"Wait." Madame Dupree raises her finger. "It's coming back to me. Something about a party and surprising someone…"

Should I remind her? But if I do, can she even handle all these plans?

"Something to do with you and your sister. Yes?"

"Uh yes, but—"

"I remember now." Madame Dupree's eyes light up. "After we collect the phones on Sunday, you can sneak in here like a little mouse. I can give you Alison's phone to call her friends. Voila. What fun. But now I must find my old dessert recipes."

While I'm still standing at the door wondering if I can leave, she heads over to a bookcase. She pulls out an ancient brown book and blows off years of dust.

"Oh, my," she says while coughing. "It's been so long since I baked any pastries." She touches the cover gently. "This was my mother's cookbook. I had hoped to leave it to my daughter." She shakes her head. "But all I have is a nephew—and he doesn't care for baking. He lives in the city and all he does is work, work, work."

I look curiously at the book. "It looks a hundred years old."

"Could be." Madame Dupree laughs. She opens it and the binding cracks. Loose pages flutter all over the floor.

"I'll get them for you," I say. As I gather the delicate faded pages, I think of my mom and Sundays. That was the day we always baked chocolate chip cookies together. We would split the dough in half—one half with the 60% cocoa chips for her and Dad, and the other batch with the regular semisweet for Alison and me. Mom told me chocolate chip cookies have a sprinkling of magic baked in them.

"Here." I hand Madame Dupree the loose pages.

"Thank you, dear." She pats my hand. "And don't forget—this Sunday after dinner. I'll be waiting here for you."

Great.

Back in our room, Suzie grills me about what happened. I guess lying is allowed when it involves a surprise party, but I cross my fingers behind my back anyway. I tell Suzie that Madame Dupree only wanted to check on my wasp bites. As soon as I mention the bites to Suzie, they start itching and stinging again. I forgot to ask how long I'm supposed to keep all this pasty stuff on my legs and arms. I figure I'll leave it on overnight.

Suzie and I head to our beds to read until bedtime. A few minutes after I climb underneath the quilt, I feel something on my leg. Must be my wasp bites. I continue reading since I'm not supposed to scratch them. But along with the itching, I now feel a tickling sensation. I throw back the cover and find a humongous black spider crawling up my leg.

I jump up screaming and it falls to the ground. Suzie runs with bare feet to the closet and grabs her sneaker. She lifts the shoe high to smack the spider.

"Don't," I shout, panicking.

Her arm stops midair. "But it's gross, why can't—"

"It might be a friend of theirs. I don't want to get them madder."

"Whose friend? What are you talking about?"

"The fair—" I catch myself. "Never mind. Just keep an eye on him." I run to the bathroom and grab two plastic cups.

"Hurry," Suzie yells. "It's crawling up the wall."

I scoop the spider into one clear cup and cover it with the other. "Got him."

Suzie runs to the window and opens it. "Let him out here."

I hesitate. *Who knows how this fairy stuff works? If it fell and died, I could be in big trouble.* "I'd rather bring him down to the garden," I say.

As I carry the cups down the three flights of stairs, I wonder about the white spider back home—and if it's still there. Meanwhile, this black one has four bubbly eyes, and they're all glaring at me through the cup. After I release him outside, he scurries into the dark. If I don't want any more creepy crawlers on me, I had better think of a present for those fairies—and soon.

CHAPTER TWELVE

Bubbling Magic in the Basement

During class the next day, I keep messing up the combinations. My turns are worse than ever and during one of the leaps, I land crooked and my ankle twists. Miss Genevieve has me sit out the rest of the class with an ice pack. While I watch from the corner, Miss Genevieve promotes Darla to the front line. Darla catches my reflection in the mirror and shoots me a toothless grin. I force a smile back and give her the thumbs up, but it's hard to watch her advancing while I make zero progress. And it's all because I'm worried about the fairies and that stupid surprise party.

By lunchtime, my ankle is feeling better. I can't find Alison or Suzie, which is okay because Oliver's the person I really need to talk to. I eat with Darla but keep darting glances at Oliver, who is sitting across the room. I'm waiting for lunch to end so I can catch up with him before he disappears with the other boys.

As soon as the bell rings, I run to the hall with the rush of other students and linger by the door. When Oliver and the other boys finally exit, they're engrossed in an animated conversation—probably comic book talk.

One of the boys catches me looking at Oliver and elbows him. "Hey, Oliver," he says with a snicker. "Your girlfriend's waiting for you."

Oliver's face reddens. "She's not my girlfriend. I'm just helping her out."

"With what?" The boy laughs.

I point to my glasses. "I wanted to ask him about an optometrist in town."

"Oh," his friend says, now looking a little guilty for his joke.

"I'll catch up with you guys later." Oliver waves them off.

"Okay. But don't forget about us. The boys here are outnumbered and we have to stick together."

After they leave, Oliver says, "I thought your glasses were all fixed."

"They are." I lower my voice. "I actually need to ask you about my bad luck because of *the you know whats.*"

"Oh, them." He glances at a couple of older students heading toward us and points down the hall. "Studio D. We can talk there."

I follow him into the large dance room. The studio is empty, except for a black baby grand in the corner. Oliver heads over and slides onto the piano stool. "So?" he says.

"You were right about the bad luck. Yesterday I got stung by a bunch of wasps." I clasp my hands together, re-sisting the urge to scratch. "I need your help figuring out what to give the fairies."

Oliver winces. "The thing is…" He places his index finger on middle C and hits it three times. *Daa daa daa.* "You have to come up with the present yourself." *Dada dada dada.* "Or it won't mean anything. And believe me, they'll know the difference."

"I don't have jewelry or anything like that. Do they like treats?"

"Of course." He acts like I should know this stuff. "Hey, do you know how to play the left-hand chords of 'Heart and Soul'?"

"My friend Lizzie taught me last summer." I sit next to Oliver. "Do you think they would like chocolate chip cookies?"

"I'm sure they would—everybody does. Just make the cookies very tiny." He points to the piano keys. "Go ahead, start."

I place my hands down and play the *bumpa da da, bumpa da da,* while Oliver plays the *daa daa daa* part. The whole time, the gift problem remains on my mind. We go through a few rounds until I stop and say, "Maybe I could bake them now."

"What?" Oliver says.

"The cookies. I don't have any more classes today." I cross my arms and tilt my head. "Do you think I could use the kitchen here?"

"Louise will ask too many questions."

"Doesn't she know about the fairies?"

"The only people that know are my grandad, Madame Dupree, and me. Everyone else thinks they're a myth." He stands and motions to the door. "You could bake them at my place. Grandad keeps our pantry stocked. In the summer it's easy to go to town for supplies, but the winter is another story."

I hadn't thought about what it must be like on the mountain in the winter. "Is the conservatory open all year?" I ask, following him out of the studio.

Oliver shakes his head. "We get too much snow up here on the mountain. The road ices up real bad."

"So what do you do all winter?"

"Grandad homeschools me, and we drive to town when the weather allows."

Oliver and I exit the conservatory through the main doors to avoid the kids in the garden, then make our way through the woods. When we pass the oak tree with a few silver dollars still shimmering inside the hollow, I remain a safe distance away and confess to Oliver how I took some coins.

"That's how you got stung?" he asks.

I nod.

A flicker of a smile crosses his lips "I can't believe you fell for that. It's a good thing you returned them."

"Uh, oh." I press my fingers to my lips.

He stops and shoots me a warning look. "Don't tell me you still have their silver dollars."

I lower my eyes from guilt. "I wasn't sure what to do with them."

He shakes his head. "You've got to learn to follow the rules in this forest."

Great. More problems. My face scrunches with worry. "Can we hurry back to the school so I can get them?"

He nods. "I think we'd better."

After we backtrack and return with the coins, I place them in a pile near the oak tree. Then we continue along the winding dirt path and come upon the weeping willow. I take a breath and stop to peek underneath. The fairies are not there. The patio furniture is still set up, but in the empty space where my glasses were, someone carved a bunch of tiny letters in the mossy dirt.

I tell Oliver to wait while I kneel for a closer look. On the first line, the letters spell out, *Làmb a bheir, 's i a gheibh.* The next line says, *Fear sam bith a loisgeas a mhàs, 's e fhèin a dh'fheumas suidhe air.*

I motion to Oliver. "Can you read this with your better than perfect vision? My eyes must be getting worse. I can't make any sense of it."

Oliver crawls under the tree and stares at the letters. "It's Gaelic." He runs his fingers through his crow-black hair. "Give me a minute to figure out the translation."

"You can read Gaelic?"

"Grandad taught me some sayings. They come in handy."

"Pretty impressive. The only foreign words I know are the French terms for our ballet steps." I wait a few minutes while Oliver studies the words. "So, what does it say?"

"Hang on, I'm trying to remember what a couple of the words mean."

While I wait, I stare at one ant carrying another on its back. The ant heads to a hole in a mound and disappears with his fallen comrade.

"Got it." Oliver nods to himself.

"Well?" I twirl a finger around my hair.

He winces. "You won't like it."

"Will you just tell me, for Pete's sake."

"Okay. The first line says, 'Whoever burns his backside must himself sit upon it.'"

"What? The fairies plan to burn my rear end?" Out of the corner of my eye, I catch a glint of tiny eyes blinking in the bushes. I gasp. I'm in a vulnerable pose, crouching over like this. I crawl out from under the tree and place my hands on my behind—for protection. "I'm afraid to ask what the second line says."

"That one's not bad. The letters spell out, 'The hand that gives is the hand that gets.'"

"I better bake those cookies before my rear suffers some horrible fate." I scan the bushes and catch more eyes blinking. "Let's get out of here."

As we hurry off, I follow Oliver along a path that veers left. After a few minutes, a log cabin in a small clearing comes into view.

"That's it," Oliver says. He raises his chin and puffs out his chest. "Neat, huh?"

"It's smaller than I thought. I pictured one of those fancy ski chalets."

His chest deflates and he lowers his eyes. "It's big enough for me and Grandad. He built it all by himself with hand-cut logs."

"Sorry, I just can't imagine living here in the woods all year long. It's so..."

"Macho?" he suggests.

"Remote," I correct. "I'm sure it's fun for a while, but it must get lonely."

"Sometimes. That's part of why Grandad has me take classes here—to make friends. The other reason is..." He pauses and grins. "I turned out to be really good at dance."

"You don't have to rub it in."

"Yeah, but it's hard, as far as the friend-making thing goes. Real friends should share secrets." His gaze darts around the forest. "I can't tell anyone about the stuff that really goes on here."

"But you told me about the fairies."

"That's because you needed my help." He takes off toward his cabin. "Come on, I thought you wanted to do some baking."

I race behind him along a dirt path, passing a large brass sundial with intersecting arcs set on a pedestal. When we reach the entrance to his cabin, I stop short. The huge moss-green front door consists of many smaller doors nailed together. Each one has separate hinges and door-knobs, and they all vary in size and color. The indigo blue door is around my height, while the buttercup yellow one comes to my waist. The one inlaid with sea glass is no taller than my knees. The smallest door, crimson and paneled with twisted twigs, barely reaches my ankles.

I scratch my head. "Not for nothing, but you sure do have a lot of doors."

He laughs. "I guess it would seem that way."

"Do they all open?"

He twists his mouth as if I've asked something absurd. "Of course." He then bends to open every door, even the tiny crimson one. They all swing open. "See?"

I tilt my head. "Adorable. But why?"

Oliver closes the doors as he answers. "After Grandad built this cabin, he found out it was on a fairy path. Since fairies come in different shapes and sizes, he built these different doors so they can all pass through. Our back door looks just like this one."

"So they just troop through your house whenever they want?"

"They're very respectful. Come on, do you want to bake those cookies or not?" He turns the nob to the human size door and swings it open. I shake my head and let out a sigh as I follow him.

Inside, the scent of cedar fills my nose. Knotty pine walls and a stone fireplace give the cabin a cozy feeling—like waking up to Christmas every morning. Now I see why Oliver likes it so much.

He leads me through the compact living room where an antique telescope on a tripod faces an open window. When we reach the kitchen, he points to a retro-red oven. "It's old, but it works great. Let's go to the pantry so you can get what you need."

While I gather all the ingredients, Oliver brings me two big bowls, a mixer, and a cookie tray. As soon as I open the chocolate chips package, Oliver rushes over, grabs a handful, and shoves them in his mouth.

"Hey, don't eat them all." I laugh and pop a few in my mouth. "I'm glad you have the semisweet ones." I follow the directions on the package, but I form the dough on the sheet into big and chunky cookies like my mom used to. While they bake, their chocolatey aroma blankets the kitchen.

"How much longer?" Oliver asks every two minutes. He pours two glasses of milk in preparation.

When they look cooked, I take them out and we wait another agonizing three minutes as they cool—slightly. There's no way we can resist warm cookies fresh from the oven, and I allow us to have two each. I'm licking my fingers when I remember I was supposed to make them tiny.

"You forgot to remind me to make them smaller. These cookies are too huge for fairies."

"Sorry." Oliver shrugs, his mouth full.

Instead of baking a whole new batch, I cut the cookies into smaller pieces and set them aside to cool. While I clean up, Oliver searches the cabin for something to wrap them in. After rummaging through closets and bureaus with no luck, he yanks on a rope from the ceiling.

"I'm going to the attic to look for holiday paper." He unfolds the ladder and climbs up. "Wait down here—it's too small for both of us."

While he's searching the attic, I explore the first floor. There's one closed door off the kitchen I haven't seen inside of yet. I turn the doorknob, expecting hanging clothes or cans of food. But this is no pantry or closet. It's a dark paneled foyer, empty except for a marble table with a bronze skull perched on top. A chill lifts the hairs on my arms and neck.

Who displays something like this in a hall leading to nowhere? First, the crazy front door, and now this? My pulse quickens, but it doesn't stop me from reaching out and touching the smooth skull. As soon as I place my hand on it, the skull slowly rotates to face me. I gasp and jump back. A second later, a clunking sound echoes in the narrow room. It's followed by a *click, click, click*, like gears spinning, and one of the paneled walls creaks open. I gasp and freeze.

Something bangs on the ceiling right above me and I stifle a yelp before remembering Oliver is searching the attic. I swallow hard and step forward, peeking into the space where the wall once was. In its place are winding stairs, leading to a basement. I bite my lip. *Should I?*

I remember an expression I heard Mom say once: "In for a penny, in for a pound." I'm sure she wasn't talking about sneaking into a creepy basement, but I can't help my nosiness from kicking in. I flick the light switch on, take a breath, and climb down the steps.

At the bottom of the stairs, there's another door—a heavy iron one, streaked with green and blue rust. I place my hand on the metal lever but pause again. What if I upset some other mythical creature? Then again, this is Oliver's grandfather's house. The wee folk may troop through it, but it's still a human house, not some fairy lair. With my hand shaking, I pull the lever and push open the door.

Inside, strips of sunlight from high tiny windows criss-cross a vast room. Flecks of dust float and dance around what looks like an old science lab. Flasks bubble with liquids of all colors, and the whole place smells faintly of rotten eggs. Herbs, gathered in bunches, hang from the ceiling, and sitting near the far end is a monstrous furnace. Shelves lining the walls hold glass jars filled with unidentifiable objects and powdery substances.

Along the cement block wall opposite the shelves, astronomical charts and ancient paintings of labs similar to this one hang in rows. A chill runs through me as I tiptoe deeper inside and head to the long wooden counters holding the flasks and beakers. In addition to their chemical formulas, they're labeled with geometric symbols and drawings of animals like peacocks, bears, lions, and swans.

One steaming beaker bubbling with an oily green liquid shows a lizard's tongue snapping up insects. I wince and run my finger along the withered spines of books crammed in the crooked shelf next to it. A book with a gold leaf cover catches my attention, and I carefully remove it from the shelf. The title is another mysterious symbol, and the musty pages contain more cryptic codes and drawings. One painting shows a rooster pecking at a fox who is devouring another rooster. Another page is a drawing of a white eagle and a red dragon, fighting in a stormy black sky swirling with hideous creatures.

"What are you doing here?"

"Gah!" I jump, bumping a flask with my elbow. Luckily, I catch it before it breaks. The moldy orange substance inside labeled *Dying Egg* would've made a huge mess.

Oliver's standing in the doorway, hands on his hips. "This room is off limits," he says sternly. He looks genuinely upset.

Heat flashes across my face. "I… I'm… I'm sorry," I stammer, placing the flask back on the table next to the oily green one.

Oliver doesn't move. "It's not safe. If that flask fell to the floor, who knows what would've happened."

"What is all this?" I ask, my voice tense.

"I'll tell you after you get out. I don't need you blowing up the cabin." He waits until I exit ahead of him, then follows me upstairs through the secret wall and foyer. A heap of wrapping paper sits outside the door to the secret hallway. Oliver shuts the door firmly, then picks up the rolls and places them on the table.

"I really am sorry. I know I shouldn't have gone down there. But since you told me everything else about this place, I was curious. I didn't think it would do much harm." I bite my lips, hoping he'll accept my apology.

Oliver sighs and lets his shoulders relax. "All right, just promise you won't tell anyone."

I stick out my pinky and he hooks his in mine. "I promise," I say.

"Okay," he says, releasing my hand. "It's Grandad's secret room. He dabbles in alchemy."

"Alchemy? I've heard of that. It's like part magic, part science, right?"

He nods. "It goes back to medieval times. It comes in handy around here. Did you see the flask with the green oily liquid?"

I nod. "Yeah."

"That's what I use for my bubble wand. Grandad makes it for me."

"Aren't you a little old for bubbles?" I tease.

"I don't do it for fun. I do it to keep the tatters away," he says defensively.

"What on earth is a tatter?"

"Certain weather brings them out. They're like mosquitos, except when they bite, they give you a tattoo." He rolls up his sleeve. "See?"

When I lean in, I see dotted lines that form patterns on his upper arm. "What does it mean?"

"I have no idea. But Grandad studied it with his microscope. It's some kind of infinite fractal—the way the shapes repeat smaller and smaller. He thinks it could hold the secret to the galaxy formation."

"All that from a bug bite?" I squint closer at the complex patterns. "Did it hurt?"

"Oh yeah. That's why I use the bubble spray—to keep them away."

"Your grandfather has tons of books in that lab. Do they have the formulas to do all that stuff?"

He nods. "My great-grandad passed them down to us. Some of them go back a few centuries."

"There was one, a gold book, with a painting of a red dragon and a white eagle. They were fighting in some ominous black sky with—"

"Evil creatures swirling around?" he finishes.

I nod. "What's all that about?"

"Grandad said that in olden times, alchemists used their own symbols and drawings to represent ingredients in their recipes. That's how they kept their chemicals a secret. He's taught me some things, but I forgot what the white eagle meant. I remember the red dragon was nitric acid. It has red vapors that devour anything in its path. I think they were fighting the evil in the sky. Did you notice that one droplet in the painting?"

I think about it, then shake my head. "I missed that."

"It's so tiny you have to really look. Grandad never figured out what it meant—probably some other secret chemical."

One roll of wrapping paper shifts then tumbles off the table, reminding me why we came here in the first place. "Thanks for finding this stuff," I say to Oliver as I pick a shiny silver paper with red bells and a small gift box.

After we finish wrapping the cookies, we head through the woods to the fairies' weeping willow. Oliver assures me my chocolate chip cookies are so scrumptious, they'll put me in excellent favor with the fairies. When we reach the willow tree, Oliver stands nearby and waits. I scan the bushes for fairy eyes. I don't see any, but I'm still worried about bending over.

"I've got a present," I shout. "I'll just leave it here for you." I scoot underneath, quite pleased with my delicious offering. But the fairy furniture is gone—every last twig. All that remains is the Gaelic warning. And they've added three exclamation points. "Uh-oh," I moan.

Oliver ducks underneath the branches. "What's wrong?"

"They're not here anymore."

"So much for your good favor."

I shake my head. "What am I supposed to do now?"

"I guess leave the cookies there anyway. Maybe they'll come back and find them."

I sigh. "I sure hope so."

After we crawl out, I turn to head back toward the school, but Oliver stops me. "Wait, don't go," he says in a shy tone. "If you stick around, I can show you something that's a big secret."

A secret? I had planned to practice my *pirouettes*, but now I'm intrigued. "What is it?"

He hesitates a second. "They're old gravestones."

I tilt my head. "Gravestones?"

"Don't you want to see them?"

I'm not so sure I do, but Oliver is already heading away, motioning me to follow.

CHAPTER
THIRTEEN

The Tree of Decayed Dreams

When we reach the lake, Oliver points to the other side. "There's a spooky old graveyard over there. I'll take you."

"But Madame Dupree said we're not allowed to—"

"Don't worry, you're safe with me." He walks along the shoreline where the two wooden rowboats I saw before are pulled up on the bank. He shoves the red one into the water and says, "Hop in."

"Wait." I pause. "Who owns that brown boat?"

"That's Grandad's."

I take a deep breath. That odd *nercited* feeling has returned, tingling deep inside of me. Even though I know I shouldn't, I climb in. After Oliver gives the boat another push from the bank, he jumps in and grabs both oars. I've never rowed before, but I offer to help.

"You sure?" he asks.

I nod. "How hard can it be?"

"Be my guest." Oliver motions to change seats. After we do, he smirks.

"What?"

"You're facing the wrong way."

"But then I'd be backwards," I say. "How will I know where I'm going? I'm not an owl."

"Very funny. Do you want to learn or not?"

I nod.

"Okay. Take hold of the oars, knees up, arms and body forward. Now drop the oars in the water behind you and pull your upper body backward."

I try but we don't move.

He shakes his head. "Put the blades sideways in the water, not flat, and not too deep. And use your abs."

Abs? I don't think I have any.

"Keep trying," he says with an amused grin. "You're doing more grunting than moving."

After a while and more coaching, I finally get the hang of it, but it's slow going. I like it, though. The sound of the boat gliding through the smooth lake is calming after the past few stressful days.

When we reach halfway, Oliver says, "You've veered to the right too much. Try turning the boat to the left."

I flick my eyes at him. "Uh, how?"

"Never mind. You'd better let me do it. I'd like to get there while we're still young."

"Thanks a lot," I say and switch seats with him.

"Watch as I turn. You can use both oars and move them in opposite directions." He demonstrates while explaining. "Or use just one and paddle it like a canoe. "See?"

Working alone, he moves us through the water effortlessly. But the closer we get to the forbidden forest, the faster my heart beats.

When we reach the other side, Oliver drags the boat onto the muddy shore and points straight ahead. As I climb out, a chill creeps down my back. Somehow, the forest on this side already feels different.

"This way," he says.

Up ahead, a hawk-like bird swoops in for a landing on a black locust tree. The hungry-eyed bird fixes its neon-green gaze on us, studying our every move.

After a few steps, Oliver stops and leans against an oak tree. "One second." He removes his left sneaker, shakes it, and a pebble falls out. His big toe sticks out of his sock.

While Oliver shoves his foot back into his sneaker, I glance up at the hawkish bird. It's still staring at us. I didn't notice before, but the bird has three legs.

"Don't worry about that brown slawk," Oliver says while tying his shoelace. "It doesn't go after people."

"Slawk?"

"It's the rat-gray slawk you have to watch out for—the one with blood-red eyes and huge hooked beak. It's monster sized—at least fifteen feet from tail to beak. The wingspan itself is thirty feet... and it *does* go after people."

"Wonderful," I say, trying to keep my voice light.

"Oh, one more thing—lightning bolts shoot from its eyes. But you don't have to worry now. He only comes out at midnight." He straightens and looks at me seriously. "There are a few other things I should tell you though."

"Oh goody," I say, glancing from him to this brown slawk.

Oliver's voice is grave. "When your spirit is broken or weak, you can be taken."

I flinch. "By who?"

He struggles to explain. "Your spirit can be stolen by anyone. You must never give your power away."

I laugh. Oliver must be joking with me. "What power? I don't have any powers—I'm not Wonder Woman."

"Your power is your control—control over your own thoughts. There are some who seek out the weak. Like that brown slawk—he's searching for small prey he can overtake. Never show the chink in your armor."

"What about the hole in your sock?" I grin.

Oliver's face reddens. "I mean it. I grew up in these woods. I know all the birds and animals that live here. I've heard the stories the trees whisper at night. And Grandad taught me all about the spirits of the dead."

That catches my attention. "There are spirits here?"

"If you listen closely at midnight, you'll hear a faint bell chime twelve times. You can only hear it in the forest. It's when the dead come out."

"But who are these spirits?"

"Grandad says they're souls who lost themselves in illusions and fell into despair. Life got to be too much for them."

"How do you get lost in an illusion?" I ask.

Oliver has to think about it. "According to Grandad, life doesn't always turn out the way people plan. He says some folks can't handle that." He runs ahead. "Come on already, I'll show you their graves!"

As soon as Oliver disappears into the forest, the brown slawk flaps its wings and fixes its neon-green eyes on me. It's not a good feeling. "Wait up," I yell. As I follow him between gnarled trees, a mist creeps through the forest. These woods smell more like almonds mixed with bitter herbs than like the piney Christmas scent on the other side of the lake. When I ask Oliver about it, he tells me it's the smell of death. I think he's only half joking.

"Check this out." Oliver points to a dead tree looming ahead.

I squint at the black silhouette in the mist. Dozens of shoes hang from the twisted, leafless branches. They remind me of sneakers tossed onto telephone wires. When we get closer, my back stiffens. The shoes are not sneakers. They're pointe shoes. But they're not pink and satiny. They're black and rotting.

"Grandad calls it the Tree of Decayed Dreams," Oliver whispers.

I move closer and reach for one, but hesitate. "What are they doing here? Who do they belong to?"

"I'll show you. But stay near me—there's poison ivy and stinging nettle around here."

"I don't like the sound of any of that."

"Don't worry, no one's going to bother you right now. Just watch out for the plants."

"What about the fairies? Do they have powers here? Because if they don't find my cookies, they'll make sure I brush up against every poisonous plant around."

"The wee folk don't like to come here." His voice is matter-of-fact again.

"I don't blame them," I mutter.

As we head forward, I repeat to myself, "Leaves of three, let them be." But I have no clue what poison nettle looks like. A strange sound interrupts my nasty plant worries. "Do you hear that humming?" I peer around. "Not more wasps…"

"No, it's coming from the graves. It always sounds like that here." We reach a rusty iron fence with a narrow gate. Oliver unhooks the metal hatch and gives it a hard shove. The hinges squeal as the gate scrapes open.

My breath catches. I expected a manicured cemetery with lots of bright green grass and plastic flowers—not dozens of crooked headstones and broken statues. They're unloved and forgotten, tangled and overgrown with thorny bramble and weeds. I've never seen a cemetery like this, so untamed and wild, claimed by the forest.

I remain frozen by the entry. "Who were these people?"

"Lost souls," Oliver says, a shadow crossing his face. "Those rotting black pointe shoes belong to the ballerinas buried here."

My throat goes dry.

"Don't be afraid. You can come in."

"I'd rather stay here."

"The dead can't hurt you now—only at night. Come on, I want to show you something."

I shake my head.

Oliver starts clucking. "Chicken."

"Fine. But only because you helped me with my cookies."

"Just watch where you step. If you see any hollow areas, avoid them. In some spots the graves have sunken."

"Thanks. I'll keep that in mind. Getting sucked into a grave would be quite inconvenient." I take a couple of steps forward, eyes on the ground, and smack into a spider web. "Yech," I say as I wipe the sticky threads off my face.

"Grandad told me that hundreds of years ago, people used spider webs to stop bleeding."

"Thanks for that bit of info, but I prefer band aides."

Sticky strings of the cobweb cling to my glasses, so I remove them and clean them with my shirt. While I have my glasses off, misty figures come into view. The billowing shapes hover over the graves. I shove my glasses back on, and the apparitions disappear.

"What's wrong?" Oliver asks. "You're white as a ghost."

"It was only my blurry vision—making shapes out of nothing."

"You do have those two different colored eyes. Remember what I said?"

"About seeing both realms?"

Oliver nods.

I shiver. "I'd rather not see anything I'm not supposed to. I'll just keep my thick purple glasses on."

As we weave through the graveyard, I read the inscriptions carved in some of the stones. The dates of death go back to the early nineteen hundreds. Green lichen and black algae have overtaken most of the older stones, making many of the names impossible to read. All the stones are a few feet high, except for one towering monument at the far end. Draped over that headstone, a marble angel weeps in despair. I move closer to read the engraving, but the vines snaking around the stone block the name.

"Whose grave is this?" I ask.

Oliver shakes his head. "That's a sad story. The woman who founded this school was Madame Valinsky. This is—"

"Oh, your grandpa told me about her. This is her grave?"

"Her daughter's," he corrects.

I brush dirt off the headstone and push the vines away to read the inscription: *Where She Fell. Our precious daughter, Priscilla Valinsky. Born 1907. Died 1923.*

Oliver points to the dates. "She was only sixteen. After she died, Madame Valinsky and her husband sold the conservatory. It broke their hearts to stay here."

"I didn't hear the full story about Priscilla—your grandpa just said it was tragic. What happened?"

"People say Priscilla was a beautiful ballet dancer, always happy—until she fell for some guy. It turned out he was only using her, and when she found out their engagement was a lie, she ran off into these woods. They say her broken heart caused her to go mad, and she danced in such a crazy frenzy she died."

"That's horrible."

"Have you heard of the ballet *Giselle*?"

I shake my head.

"You should read up on it. The conservatory has books about all the famous ballets in the library. Anyway, Priscilla's not the only one here who died from a broken heart." Oliver motions to the rest of the graves. "They all did."

I glance around at the old stone markers. "Are they all girls?"

"Yeah," he says, his voice quiet and tense. "I mean, I don't want to creep you out, but you asked." He pauses, then points to a clearing in the woods outside the cemetery. "You see that knoll over there? Every night the Wilis in these graves rise at midnight and dance until dawn."

My spine stiffens. If fairies exist in these woods, then maybe these otherworldly beings do also. "What are they called again?"

"You spell it W-i-l-i-s, but pronounce it Willies."

"Like when someone says, 'That gives me the willies'?"

"Exactly. They're ghost sylphs—winged air spirits. They never age. Grandad says I'm safe from them for a couple of years. Kids have some sort of protection from still being innocent or something like that. But after a few more birthdays, he says I'll become vulnerable to their powers."

"What kind of powers?"

"Apparently these Wilis cast some kind of spell on dudes. As soon as a guy dances with them, it's all over." Oliver draws a finger across his throat for emphasis and I shudder. He then glances up at the sun's position in the sky. "It's getting late. We'd better go."

"Wait," I say. "What happened to the guy who lied to Priscilla?"

Oliver looks straight at me. "People say his body is rotting at the bottom of the lake—along with the rest of the guys."

I take in a sharp breath. "What guys?"

"The ones who broke the other ballerinas' hearts. It's not even safe for certain girls to come here at night."

I swallow. "Which girls?"

"Legend says if a girl comes here with a broken heart, she'll never return. The Wilis dance with them all night until dawn. Then the Wilis return to these graves and drag the new girl down with them. The girl dies and becomes one of them for eternity. It's like they have a deadly sisterhood.

Some sort of lonely hearts club. They're always looking to recruit more souls."

"What about that tree—"

"The Tree of Decayed Dreams?"

I nod.

"The jilted girls give the Wilis their earthly slippers before dancing to death."

"You're freaking me out." The cemetery is getting darker by the minute and I peer at a gaping hole in the ground. It looks like it's waiting for someone. "Has anyone ever escaped?"

"This isn't in Grandad's books, so I don't know if it's true, but I heard a story about one girl. She ran screaming through the woods and got away somehow. They say she made it out just before dawn." He pauses. "The only thing is…"

I'm all anticipation. "The only thing is what? Tell me."

"The Wilis punished her for getting away. Her toes turned blue, then black, and then they cracked off. After that, she could never dance again."

Gross. "What a nice story. Thanks for sharing."

"You asked. Grandad said that was a shame because her feet could have been saved if she caught it before her toes turned completely blue."

"How?"

"By holding a rose quartz crystal in one hand and citrine in the other while soaking her feet in the lake. Grandad said rose quartz heals emotional pain and citrine takes care of the physical ones. And the lake holds its own secret magic."

I roll my eyes. Now I know he's kidding with me. "Well sure, everybody has those exact crystals lying around the house."

"Grandad does. He has a bunch of them."

Of course he does. "So he believes the story is true? My dad takes me to the annual gem and fossil show at our fairgrounds. I love looking and touching all of the crystals, but I never thought they really had any powers."

Oliver shrugs. "Maybe you don't, but a lot of people do. Besides, he doesn't tell me everything he believes. I guess I'm on a need-to-know basis." He heads to the cemetery gate. "Come on—we better go before it gets dark."

"Sounds good to me. I've had enough of this place."

We hurry through the twisted trees to Oliver's boat and climb in. As he pushes the boat off shore, I glance back at the forbidden forest, glad to leave it behind. But while Oliver rows, a moaning wind swirls across the lake and curls around our tiny boat. In the depths of the green lake, dark shadows take on sinister shapes. A floating branch resembles a skeletal hand, reaching out for help. I beg Oliver to row faster while I try not to think about what—or who—lurks beneath.

When we reach the other side, I relax for a moment. But as I climb out of the boat, tiny eyes hiding in the woods blink at me. Since Oliver doesn't say anything, I try to ignore them. As Oliver and I hurry forward, we pass the fairies' willow tree. Their miniature furniture is still gone, and now, so are my cookies.

"I hope the fairies found them and not some other woodland creature," I say.

Oliver shrugs. "You didn't catch any poison ivy or get any more bug bites, so you might be safe."

The word "might" stays in my head the rest of the way back.

When we reach the conservatory, Oliver joins the other boys outside shooting hoops and I head to the library. As soon as I open the thick oak-paneled door, a musky leather scent fills my nose. The hushed empty room glows with an orange hue from the stained-glass windows. No one else is inside. Shelves of books on ballet line the walls, and after scanning past volumes on *Sleeping Beauty*, *The Nutcracker*, and *Cinderella*, I find a book on *Giselle*. With the book in hand, I head to a reading table and pull the brass chain of its green lamp. I take a deep breath and start reading:

Giselle is a ballet about a beautiful young peasant who lives in a European country village. One day a handsome nobleman comes to town and courts her. She falls in love with him, not knowing he is engaged to another woman. When she learns of his deception, she is devastated. She runs into the woods at night and comes upon the Wilis. These winged ghost-sylphs are young women who died from broken hearts, doomed to grieve through eternity. Rejected before their wedding day, they hold a vengeance against all men. Every night at the stroke of midnight, they rise from their graves and dance in their bridal gowns until dawn. The Wilis initiate Giselle into their sisterhood and she dances all night to her death.

First, a gamekeeper searches for Giselle. But any man who approaches the Wilis falls under their spell. Powerless to resist, the gamekeeper is lured to his doom by the Wilis and thrown into the lake. When the nobleman comes next, he proclaims his true love and begs Giselle to forgive him. But Giselle is now a ghost-sylph, and the queen of the Wilis commands Giselle to dance him to his death. In older versions, the nobleman falls from exhaustion and dies, but in newer ones, Giselle forgives him and the curtain closes as he cries over her grave.

I pause for a minute to study the pictures. The ballerinas are dressed in long white tutus with wispy veils covering their faces. Since the original story took place in Europe, that must mean the Wilis exist in secret forests all over the world.

I think about what Jeremiah told Oliver—that in a few years Oliver would lose his protection against the powers of the Wilis. As I close the book, Alison comes to mind. She's at that age now, and it's like she's fallen under Dylan's spell. Her every mood depends on him. I think of her as BD (Before Dylan) Alison—my fun sister—and AD (After Dylan) Alison—my distant, moody sister. I'm glad I'm still immune to all that.

As I place the book back on the shelf, a heavy encyclopedia falls to the ground, hitting my pinky toe. "Ow," I yelp and pick up the book. The elf-green cover fits its title: *Faeries You May Come Upon.* Interesting. I search through the worn pages, wondering if any flower fairies are in there. Midway through, I come upon an illustration that looks like the one I drew. It's in a section called "The Good Faeries." That's a relief.

But before I replace the book, I can't resist flipping through the second part: "The Not-So-Good Faeries." Towards the back, I find a picture of something familiar— blue flickering lights, floating above a lake. My eyes widen as I read about them.

Will-o'-the-Wisps lure travelers into the dark, often into danger. Their appearance can also be a sign of someone's death.

They look like the lights floating by Alison's window that first night. But that can't be. She never even mentioned seeing them. I bet they were only a swarm of weird upstate bugs. Maybe Alison or her roommate left some candy by the window. Sweets attract all kinds of insects. That had to be it. I slam the book shut and shove it back on the shelf.

When I head back to my room, Suzie asks if I want to play charades. While we take turns acting out a bunch of movies and books, I struggle to concentrate. The images of the Wilis from the library book remain in my head. When we get tired of acting, Suzie brings one of her books to her bed and starts reading. I grab my sketchbook and colored pencils and head to my desk.

First, I draw the Wilis with their white veils. Then I sketch the blue floating Will-o'-the-Wisps. As I'm about to put my pad away, my hand starts drawing almost on its own. As the shapes form, I realize they're from that painting in Jeremiah's gold book—the one with the white eagle and red dragon, attacking the black cloud of monsters. When I finish, I remove all three drawings and spread them out on my bed. As I study them, a shudder runs through me.

"What were you drawing?" Suzie asks from her bed.

"Nothing," I say, quickly hiding them in the pad.

CHAPTER FOURTEEN

The City People Are Here

On Sunday we have no classes, and Madame Dupree arranges a trip to town for the students. Jeremiah's bus only seats around half the students, so he makes two runs. Suzie and I ride on the first trip, while Oliver and the boys go on the second. Alison is on my bus, but she sits with the older girls in the rear. A rumor floats around the bus about an upcoming party. I keep quiet and wonder if someone overheard Madame Dupree talking to Louise or Jeremiah. During the ride, Suzie grills me about what Oliver and I did yesterday. I only tell her about exploring the woods on the safe side of the lake.

When we arrive in town, the teachers and students split into groups depending on where they want to shop. Suzie decides to browse the costume jewelry store with some of the Pixie As. While I debate whether to pick the old-fashioned candy store or the used bookstore, Alison taps me on the shoulder.

"Hey, Squeak. Want to go clothes shopping with me?"

A big smile spreads across my face. "I'd love to," I say, jumping at the chance to spend time with her.

There are no malls in Faylinn, but a number of boutiques line Main Street. Alison picks out one called the Three Wishes Boutique, and as I follow her inside, she says, "We should both buy something nice for the party."

Oh no. I hope she didn't find out about the surprise. "Party?" I say, playing dumb.

She nods. "I hear Madame Dupree is planning an open house party."

"Oh," I say, relieved.

"Come on." She grabs my hand. "Dad gave us extra spending money. Let's see what they've got here."

We head deeper into the store toward the racks with my size. "Oh, look," she says, lifting a dress covered in large polka dots. "Your favorite. Why don't you try it on?"

I take it from her and hold it up. It is cute.

A smile tugs at her lips. "I bet Oliver will like that on you."

I feel my face flush.

"I heard you two have been spending a lot of time together."

I shove the dress back. "It's nothing like that. He's just a friend."

She smirks. "Okay, okay. But you should buy that dress anyway. It'll look great on you." She then rummages through the racks with her size and picks up a flowery boho style dress. "What do you think?" She holds it to her shoulders and spins around. "Oh look, it comes with a matching scarf."

"It's pretty," I say as I study her mood. I'm wondering if she's heard from Dylan, but I don't ask.

"Let's try them on." Alison says, heading to the dressing room.

I grab the polka-dotted dress, and as I follow her, I start fretting about the phone calls I have to make later. I hope Mr. Too Cool comes to her surprise party, but I also don't want him to ruin it if he does come. While I'm slipping the dress on, I realize I don't have a present for Alison's birthday. While she's still in the dressing room, I change back into my clothes and run around the store, searching for something to get her. Before I find anything, she comes out.

"You ready, Squeak?" she says.

"I guess." I'm upset that I missed my chance to buy her a present. But it's too late now.

After Alison and I pay for our new dresses, we head to the ice cream shop. Some of the other students are inside, including Oliver, who's sitting in the back with the boys. Alison winks at me when she sees him, but I ignore her. Alison and I sit in a booth at the front, and little Darla joins us. Between spoonfuls of chocolate, I sneak peeks toward the back of the room. Oliver's head of thick black hair is lowered, immersed in his vanilla sundae. The blond kid next to him keeps scratching a splattering of red blisters across his face and neck. They don't look like bites, but I'm not sure what they could be from. When Oliver turns to talk to the boy to his other side, the blond kid tastes Oliver's sundae.

I shake my head and return to my own ice cream. Boys are weird.

At dinner that night, Jeremiah and Louise collect everyone's cellphones again. That's my signal to head to Madame Dupree's office. I eat slowly until I'm one of the last ones in the dining hall, and I tell Suzie not to wait for me. When I'm done eating and no one else is around, I walk to Madame's office near the front entrance and knock. No one answers. Outside, a car door slams. I glance through an open window at the shiny black Mercedes parked at the entrance.

A man in crisp white shorts with a sky-blue sweater tied around his neck opens the passenger door. A woman struts out in heels at least five inches high. She's dressed all in white—like she's stepped out of a magazine ad for some ritzy resort. She yells something at the man, and he rushes to open the trunk. While he yanks out two designer suitcases and one duffle bag, she removes a gold compact mirror from her snakeskin purse and examines her reflection. She powders her nose, then snaps the mirror closed and bends to extract a bouquet of flowers from the back seat of the car.

Down the hall, the rec room door swings open, and I duck into the closest door to avoid being seen by whoever is coming out. I walk smack into a broom and somehow catch it before it clatters to the ground, giving me away. I freeze as Darla walks past the crack in the door, then gently rest the broom back against the wall. Of course I'd hide in a broom closet.

I'm just about to step out when the sound of the front doors swishing open is followed by the rapid clicking of high heels down the hall towards me.

"So you agree you'll talk to her. Right, sweetie?" The smooth voice must be the woman I saw outside, and a moment later she and the man walk into my line of sight through the cracked door.

"Honey, I never said that. You know my aunt loves this place," the man is saying gently. He takes her arm and she stops, turning to face him. They're feet away from the closet. I try to breathe quietly.

"We'd only be helping her," the woman says. "I care about her as much as you do."

He pauses. "I'm only here for a nice visit."

"You'll be inheriting all this anyway." The woman gestures with a dismissive hand, gold rings glinting on two fingers. "This way you would just get it sooner."

The scent of the flowers she's holding wafts toward me, and I feel a sneeze build. I hold my breath and close my eyes. *Please don't sneeze...*

"Think of all the money we could get from selling it now," the woman continues, her voice syrupy. "Developers would love to snap up all this land. And it would be great for her too. She could get a condo in Florida. Maybe overlooking the ocean and—"

"She hates the heat."

The sneeze feeling passes and I exhale in relief, opening my eyes.

"Sweetie, that's not the point. You'd be doing her a favor. She could retire and move anywhere. And so could we. You know she's too old to keep running this place." The woman's voice is getting sharper, and now her hand is on her hip.

"That's up to her to decide," he says in a strained tone. "We should get settled and unpack."

A ringing interrupts the woman, who had opened her mouth to reply, and she digs around in her purse to pull out her cell phone. She glances at its screen, then looks up with a big smile.

"What great news." She touches the man's arm and kisses his cheek. "My realtor found us a fantastic apartment."

His forehead pinches together. "I have an apartment."

I'm starting to feel antsy. How long will I have to stay in this stuffy closet? It would look ridiculous for me to pop out now.

"But this one's on Park Avenue. We could move in right after we get married. That is, if your aunt would—"

"But—"

"Sweetie, if I left things up to you, we'd still be driving around in your old Corolla."

"At least it was paid for." He shifts the suitcases, his body drooping from their weight.

"I'm sorry," she says, squeezing his arm again. "You're tired. We can talk about this later. Where's our room?"

"We're up on the fourth floor—room forty-nine."

She looks up and down the hall. "Which way to the elevator?"

He laughs. "There is no elevator."

"Just like your apartment," she says and moves down the hallway toward the staircase.

When I can no longer hear her high heels or the man's shoes shuffling after her, I step out of the closet. As I glance down the empty hall, a lingering scent from the woman's flowers fills my nose.

Who were those people?

I push them out of my mind and head back to Madame Dupree's office. I knock again, but still no one answers. After a moment, I step inside. "Madame Dupree?" But the room is empty. While I wait, I straighten the old ballet photos on the wall.

Right when I've decided Madame Dupree has forgotten about our meeting, she breezes in carrying a bouquet of flowers. "I'm so sorry, dear. My nephew, Adam, and his fiancée, Clarissa, just arrived. Adam is my only living relative, so it is always such a treat to see him. And Clarissa brought me these lovely yellow roses." She takes a whiff before setting them on her desk.

"Now, I know you and I had an appointment today, but for the life of me, I can't remember what it was about." She frowns. "Can you remind me?"

She really is getting forgetful. "The surprise party for my sister, Alison. You wanted me to call two of—"

"Ah yes. Come, we'll find her phone in the mail slots." Madame Dupree leads me down the hall to a large storage room. As she unlocks the door, she asks what my last name is.

"MacAdoo." I spell it out for her.

"Of course," she says. "Now I remember." She rummages through the alphabetized slots and hands me Alison's phone. "I have no clue how to work these things." She smiles. "I guess I've been alive too long."

I stare at the phone, wondering whether to call Dylan or Mila first. "Can the guests stay here?"

She shakes her head. "They would have to make their own arrangements."

That solves that. Neither one will come now, but I still need to make the effort. I decide to call Mila first. Alison has Mila's name saved as BFF. I press her number and two rings later, Mila picks up.

"Hey Alison," Mila says. "What's up?"

"It's Kiki." I explain why I'm using Alison's phone and tell her about the surprise party. "But since you can't stay here, I guess you won't be able to come," I say. "Right?"

"Actually, my parents have a ski lodge in the next town over from Mount Faylinn. That's why I went to the conservatory the last two summers."

"Really?" I say, deflated. "I'm supposed to invite Dylan also, but—"

"My uncle's vacationing at the lodge for the summer, so if Dylan wants, he can stay there also. I'll call him now and get right back to you."

A few minutes later, Mila calls back. She says that she and Dylan will both come to the party. I tell her about the open house cover, and to say she can't come if Alison calls to ask her or Dylan to be her guest.

"Wonderful," Madame Dupree says when I tell her the news.

So it's happening. And I still don't have a present for Alison.

That evening as I dig through my bag looking for a missing sock, I find a photo of Alison from our spring recital. I forgot I had it buried in my dance bag. She's wearing a mint-green ballet costume, posed in an *arabesque*. An idea lights up my brain, and I rip off a fresh paper from my sketchpad, open my tin of colored pencils, and start drawing.

CHAPTER
FIFTEEN
Balancing on Bowlegs

The next day, Madame Dupree summons everyone to the theater auditorium for two announcements. I file into a seat next to Suzie, assuming one of the announcements concerns the open house party, which is really the surprise party. I'm right. Madame Dupree says that each person can invite two guests. The second announcement is that one week after the open house, on the last day of camp, all the classes will participate in a ballet performance here onstage. We don't have time to practice a full ballet during the three-week camp, so it will just be a shorter presentation for the parents.

My mind races. A presentation? Even a short one involves dancing on stage in front of everyone. And Dad will be back from Australia by then. So now I have another worry. Dad spent good money for me to come here, and so far, I haven't improved one iota. I'd better start practicing and paying more attention in class.

Before we leave the auditorium, Madame Dupree asks if there are any questions. Suzie raises her hand. "How can we invite anyone to the open house without our cell phones?"

Madame Dupree remains silent a moment and then laughs to herself. "Oh my, you're right dear. I overlooked that little detail. I'll have them returned to you today after dinner for one hour."

Louise hands out the phones after dinner, and soon after Alison finds me. "Is there anyone you want to call, Squeak?"

I hadn't even thought about that. "The only friend I can think of is Lizzie, but she's away at baseball camp."

"I'm going to invite Mila and Dylan. I can't wait for him to see me in that new dress." Alison rushes to the stairs. "I'll be right back."

I head to the parlor and plop down on the velvet sofa while I wait for Alison to return. She's all happy now, but after Mila and Dylan tell her they can't make it, Alison will get upset. This is why I hate parties, especially surprise ones.

Alison returns a few minutes later, her head slumped. "They can't make it."

I give her a hug. "Their loss."

During the next few days, I try to push the surprise party, the presentation, the fairies, and the Wilis out of my mind. Otherwise, my head will explode. I came here to work on my dancing. I have to focus.

Darla continues to improve, which frustrates me more than ever. Miss Genevieve reminds us to concentrate on ourselves, but I can't help comparing myself to the other girls in my class. It's not fair how things come easier to some of them. During one of our combinations, I psych myself up and attempt a triple *pirouette*. I push off too hard during the preparation from fourth position and throw my center way off balance. During the second rotation, I fall on my rear end. As the room erupts in laughter, I see my face turn strawberry red in the mirror.

Miss Genevieve claps her hands. "Girls, that's enough."

Darla shoots the laughing girls a stern look and heads over to help. Before she reaches me, I jump up and run out of the room, trying to hold back tears.

A moment later, Miss Genevieve finds me in the hall and gently takes my hand. "I never want you to stop pushing yourself, Kiki. That's the only way to improve. You have so many years ahead of you. If you keep working and practicing, you'll surprise yourself with what you can do." Her tone is kind and encouraging.

I lower my head. "But some of the girls are so much better than—"

She squeezes my hand to stop me. "That may be true. But many students born with natural talent take it for granted and throw it away. You, my dear, will never take anything you accomplish in dance, and hopefully in life, for granted. After class today, I'll show you special exercises and techniques to practice on your own." She lifts up my chin with her manicured finger. "Now, think of something that makes you happy and give me one of your beautiful smiles."

An image of my mother hugging me in her polka-dotted apron comes into my head. I remember how she once told me that we all fall on our behinds—figuratively and literally. When I think of the word *literally* and how Alison got the meaning all wrong, I grin. But now, I've forgotten what *figuratively* means.

"That's much better." Miss Genevieve smiles back and points to the dance room. "Are you ready to return to class?"

I nod and follow her into the studio. When we enter, Miss Genevieve admonishes the girls who laughed, reminding them we should support one another. After class, she shows me how to work on my balance and core by standing at the barre on one leg, with the other foot pointed to the side of my knee in *passé*. She tells me to rise to *relevé* and hold that position. Because of my bowlegs and weak ankles, I have to adjust my center of balance when standing on one leg. I'm not a natural turner, but she assures me I will improve with practice.

After she leaves, I remain alone in the studio. As I *relevé* on the other foot, Oliver walks in.

"Hey." I grin. "What are you doing here?"

He halts by the entry. "Sorry. I thought the room was empty. I was going to work on my jumps."

When he doesn't smile back, I feel a ping in my stomach. Maybe I upset him the last time we hung out. "I haven't seen you around," I say, trying to sound casual. "What's up?"

"My group's been practicing like crazy and I guess I've been feeling a bit rundown." He rubs his forehead.

"Oh," I say, relieved and still balancing on *relevé*. "I guess you heard about the open house party. Did you invite anyone?"

He shakes his head. "I'm homeschooled—I don't have any friends outside of dance." He turns silent for a moment. "Well... I guess I'll leave you alone to practice."

"Wait." I rush over to him. "Are you angry at me for some reason?"

He stops and gives me a confused look. "No, why?"

"I don't know. You seem different—kind of distant."

He lets out a long sigh. "It's not you. It's my grandad."

"What's wrong? Is he sick?" I ask anxiously.

"No, it's nothing like that. But ever since Madame Dupree's relatives arrived, he's been acting really worried. But he won't tell me why."

I think of Little Miss Priss and all her luggage. "Do you know her relatives?"

"I never met them."

"I saw them the other day. Her nephew's name is Adam, and Clarissa is his fiancée." I wrinkle my nose. "That Clarissa is something else. From what I heard her say to Adam, good enough isn't good enough. She said Madame should sell the conservatory and land to developers so they can buy a new apartment."

Oliver gasps. "Developers? This is terrible! That would mean… the end of the conservatory!" He rakes his hands through his hair. "Grandad and I would have to move." His forehead creases. "I don't get it. Madame Dupree would never let go of this school."

"It sounded like it was all Clarissa's idea."

Oliver steps out to the hall and glances up and down. "Do you know where they're staying?"

"I heard them say room forty-nine."

His face goes white. "That's Priscilla's old bedroom."

A shiver crawls up my neck, but before I can say anything, the bell rings. We both have another class to attend, but we make plans to meet afterward to snoop. Oliver tells me to find the window seat on the eastern end of the fourth floor and wait there for him.

CHAPTER
SIXTEEN

Whom Do You Trust?

After class, I rush up to the fourth floor. At the landing, a musty smell hangs heavy in the air. I pause to catch my breath and look up and down the long empty hall. Which way is east? I begin wandering, figuring I'll find Oliver eventually. None of the students board on this floor, and my ears ring from the eerie silence. There are many doors, but they're all shut. When I reach room forty-nine, the air turns cold and a chill comes over me. I put my ear to the door, hold my breath, and listen. The room is silent except for a hissing sound whirring inside.

I back away, feeling unsettled. We should have met in the rec room—anywhere other than here. This room and floor give me the creeps. I hurry away down the maze of halls and spot a window bench at the far end. When I reach it, I gaze out the hazy stained-glass window onto the parking area. Steps echo behind me just as a black Mercedes drives into the lot below.

I turn to see Oliver approaching, and I beckon him over and point out the window. "Look, that's them."

Oliver rushes over. "Shoot. I wanted to sneak into their room."

"Too late for that," I say.

We watch Adam open the trunk and pull out four shopping bags. He lugs them to the conservatory door while Clarissa trails behind, carrying only her purse.

"What now?" I ask.

"We wait here and see where they go. Maybe they'll head to the kitchen first."

A few moments later, we hear footsteps climbing the stairs. Then a voice echoes down the hall. "My shoes are killing me. These four flights are too much."

"That's Clarissa," I whisper. "What should we do?"

"Just stay. If we leave now, it'll look suspicious."

"I can't wait to get back to the city. And designer stores," Clarissa whines.

"If you didn't like these shops, why'd you buy all these clothes?" Adam asks, sounding out of breath.

"The less time in our room, the better. It's so cold and clammy. There's something morbid about it."

"You asked for the biggest room," he reminds her. Their voices are getting closer.

"Uh-oh," Oliver says. "They're heading toward us. Stay cool."

"Maybe tomorrow we could drive a few towns away. See what other stores they have around here."

"How about we take a break from shopping tomorrow," Adam tells her. "You know I don't get much chance to escape the city. I'd really like to go rock climbing."

"Rock climbing?" Clarissa bursts out laughing as they turn the corner at the end of the hall and come into view.

Oliver whispers, "Pretend we're talking about dance."

I gesture my arms around like a bad actor and say, "So I'm having a hard time with my turns and—"

"Oh hello, children." Clarissa waves at us with her jeweled encrusted nails, a too-bright smile on her face as they walk toward us. "What are you two doing here? I thought the kids' rooms were on the second and third floors."

I swallow. "Uh, we—"

"We were just hanging out," Oliver says. "We didn't know anyone was staying here. We'll leave now."

"That's all right," Adam says. "Stay as long as you like. This floor is way too quiet."

The beat of silence after he finishes is broken by the ring of a cell phone. Adam struggles with the shopping bags and pulls out his phone from his back pocket. "I've got to take this," he tells Clarissa. "It's a new client."

"Go ahead, honey." Clarissa smiles. "I'll meet you back at the room in a minute."

Leaving the bags in the hall, Adam steps into their room, talking quietly into his cell. Clarissa peers down at Oliver and me. Her black-lined eyes narrow. "Can I ask you a couple of questions? You're students here, right?"

Oliver and I nod.

"Madame Dupree will be family soon and I'm concerned about her well-being. Does she... oh, I don't know, ever act strange?"

"Strange?" Oliver asks.

"You know," Clarissa says, fluttering her hand about. "Forget something important or say bizarre things—the way some seniors do?"

Oliver coughs. Either he's giving me a signal or her jasmine perfume is making him sick. "Madame Dupree is just fine," he says.

"What about you?" She fixes her eyes on me. "There must be something you can think of." When I don't say anything, she steps closer and says, "I'm only trying to help her."

Oliver nudges me with his elbow.

"Nope," I say. "Can't think of anything strange."

Clarissa sighs. "There must be—"

"We have to go," Oliver says. "We can't be late for class."

With that, Oliver and I shoot up from the window seat and sprint down the hall. As soon as we're out of earshot, Oliver whispers, "So that's what Grandad was worrying about. You're right. She wants to take everything away from Madame Dupree."

"Would you and your grandfather really have to move? Can they do that?"

"She must think they can." Oliver's voice turns sharp. "We've got to warn Madame Dupree and stop them."

Oliver and I dash down the four flights to her office and bang on her door.

"Come in," she calls.

Oliver and I rush in, panting.

She glances up from her desk. "Is everything all right?"

"We have to talk to you," Oliver says, closing the door behind us.

"Well then, have a seat." She gestures to the chairs in front of her desk, then realizes they are covered in stacks of books and paperwork. "Oh sorry, my apologies. Every day, more and more things seem to pile up. It's so hard keeping up with it all. Give me a moment." She scurries back and forth, arms full, piling everything on her desk. We offer to help, but she waves us off. By the time she sits behind her desk, the mountains of papers and books tower so high, only her eyes are visible.

"So, what is this all about?" the top of her head says.

Oliver and I wait for the other to speak.

"Well?" she says, rising from the desk. "I'm an old woman. I don't know how much longer I can wait."

Oliver nods at me.

"All right," I blurt out. I take a moment to swallow. "We came to warn you about Adam and Clarissa."

"My nephew?"

Oliver leans in and lowers his voice. "We think Clarissa wants to take the school away from you."

"What?" Madame Dupree's eyes widen, but she looks dazed and unfocused.

I nod. "It's true. I heard her talking about it."

"That can't be." Madame Dupree falls silent a moment. "Clarissa did ask if I would ever sell, and I told her no. But she and Adam would never do anything like that. He knows he's due to inherit everything anyway—on two conditions."

"What conditions?" Oliver asks.

"The same conditions my parents agreed to when they bought it from Madame Valinsky. He must continue to run the dance conservatory and to preserve all the surrounding land." Madame Dupree points to an old black-and-white photo on the wall of a ballerina. "That was my mother, Odette Dupree. My father purchased all this for her. It was a big change for them to move here from Paris, but it was her dream to run her own school."

Oliver and I examine the photo. Odette Dupree is in a classic swan pose—arched back, arms high with bent wrists and elbows. A white feathered crown covers her dark hair, framing her youthful features.

"She was beautiful," I say. "Did you grow up in Paris too?"

She shakes her head. "I was born here, but my parents spoke mostly French to me." She then touches another old photo of a woman and a teenaged girl. "And this was Madame Valinsky and her daughter Priscilla."

Priscilla is wearing a flowing white ballet skirt, posing outside in the garden. Her shoulder length hair, curled in ringlets, reminds me of a silent movie actress. "Her hair is white," I say, confused. "But she looks around Alison's age."

"She *was* Alison's age. People say her hair was ice-blond, but you can't tell from that old black-and-white photo." A shadow crosses Madame Dupree's face. "That was the last picture ever taken of her." She gazes out the window and points in the direction of the forest. "Priscilla is buried out there—on the other side of the lake." She sighs and shakes her head. "Poor Priscilla and all the other young women…"

Oliver and I lock eyes while Madame Dupree remains lost in her thoughts.

After a long moment, she turns to us with a pained look. "Well, thank you both for stopping by…"

"We know," Oliver blurts out.

"Know what, dear?" she asks with a puzzled look.

"About Priscilla and the others." He hesitates, then continues, "How they're doomed to dance every night—for all eternity."

"Oh my." Her trembling hand touches her neck. "Who told you?"

"Grandad. Last year, he caught me sneaking to that side of the lake and warned me about them."

She inclines her head gravely. "Now you understand what I've been faced with all of these years. I must say, during all my time here, I have never lost a student to the Wilis. But before me…" She tightens her lips, her face etched in worry. "If this land was sold and those graves dug up, I dread to imagine what would happen."

"Does Adam know about the Wilis and the fairies?" I ask.

"You know about the fairies also?"

We nod.

Madame Dupree's brows crease. "I've tried to tell Adam, but he thinks I'm—"

"Crazy?" Oliver says.

"Oliver." I shoot him a look. "That's not nice."

"I've tried to tell him because one day he'll inherit it all—fairies and Wilis included." Madame fiddles with her scarf. "But he just takes what I say in stride, like it's one of my eccentricities."

"I think Clarissa is behind all of this," I say.

Madame Dupree paces her small office. "I'm sure it's all a big misunderstanding. She's been nothing but kind. Remember the lovely yellow roses she brought me?" Madame points to a windowsill. The bouquet is shriveled and dead. "Oh my, I guess I forgot to put them in water."

"From now on, you have to act as normal as you can," Oliver says. "Don't let them know you forget things. And you'd better not mention the Wilis or the wee folk."

"But they're real. You both know that. Right?"

"I know that, and Kiki knows that," Oliver says. "But if you want to keep Adam and Clarissa from taking everything away, you can't talk about that stuff. If you act normal, they can't do any—"

A knock at the door interrupts him, and I glance at him. What if it's Clarissa?

"Yes?" Madame Dupree calls out.

Louise peeks her head in. "Some of the decorations for the open house have arrived."

"I'll be right there," Madame Dupree says. Louise shuts the door, and Madame turns to us. "I don't mean to cut you off, but I must check on this delivery." She shakes her head. "There's so much going on with the open house coming up, but thank you for stopping by."

As we head out, she whispers, "Don't worry so much, children. I'm sure everything is fine."

CHAPTER
SEVENTEEN

Sixteen Candles

Back-to-back intensive ballet classes fill the next few days. In the evenings, I work on my surprise drawing. I haven't seen Oliver around, but I imagine he's busy with his rehearsals also. There's no time to snoop on Adam and Clarissa, but the fate of the school still weighs on my mind.

When the morning of Alison's surprise party arrives, I wake up with a start, shivering.

"You okay?" Suzie asks. "You were thrashing around something awful in your sleep."

I rub my eyes and try to clear my head. I can't tell Suzie I dreamed the Wilis were chasing me. "Just a silly nightmare," I say and fake a yawn.

"I hate bad dreams," she says. "Better hurry so we don't miss breakfast."

While I jam my legs into my leotards and tights, Suzie chatters away about her cousin who is coming to the party tonight. I wish I could tell her the truth about everything, but I don't want her to accidentally spoil the surprise for Alison after all the work Madame Dupree put in.

During breakfast, I scan the dining hall for Oliver. Two of the other boys are sitting at the far end in their regular spot, but Oliver and the blond boy are not with them. Maybe Oliver overslept or had an early practice.

Today we have a shortened schedule due to the party. I'm supposed to keep an eye out for Dylan and Mila and make sure they don't run into Alison. The plan is for them to call Madame Dupree when they arrive in the evening, and then for me to sneak them to the old ballroom. Alison's pointe teacher, Miss Natalia, plans to keep Alison occupied in one of the dance studios while everyone gathers in the ballroom.

All of this gives me a stomachache, and during lunch and dinner, I hardly get any food down. Oliver's still not with the other boys, but I figure I'll see him later at the party.

After dinner, I find Alison and wish her a happy birthday—it's the first time I've seen her all day. I ask her to come to my room, and she follows me upstairs. When we get there, I take out the special drawing I've been working on—Alison in the mint-green costume she wore for her solo in her spring ballet recital.

"This is for you," I say, and as I give it to her, I feel myself beaming. For the first time, the hands don't look half bad.

Her eyes light up. "Oh, Kiki, it's beautiful. I love it. When we get home I'm going to frame it and hang it in my room."

"I almost forgot—I made you a card also." I run to my bureau and pull it out.

Alison reads it aloud: "Happy sixteenth birthday to the best sister in the world. Thank you for looking after me ever since Mom died. Love and kisses, Kiki." Alison presses the card to her heart and starts to cry.

"I'm so sorry." I rush over to her. "I didn't mean to make you sad."

"No, you made me very happy." She hugs me. "I know I haven't been that great a sister lately."

She's back to her old self in this moment, which makes me all lubbly jubbly inside.

"Oh, by the way, Dad texted me today. He wished me a happy birthday and said he misses and loves us and will see us in a week. I just wish he and Dylan were coming tonight."

I don't say anything back. Good old Dylan—the mood spoiler has crept back into her brain. I wish I could tell her he is coming, but she'll just have to wait and see for herself.

Alison glances at my alarm clock. "I'd better run now and change into my new dress. Miss Natalia wants me to help organize some class music before the open house starts." She gives me a kiss on the cheek. "Thanks so much for my card and present. I'll see you later."

After she leaves, I change into my new polka-dot dress and the polka-dot Mary Jane shoes I packed. As I'm about to head out the door, Suzie comes in. I make up an excuse about having to get something and hurry down to Madame Dupree's office.

When I get there, Madame Dupree is pacing. "Thank goodness you're here. Alison's friends just called. They're on their way over." She wrings her hands. "What should we do?"

"You told me to meet them outside."

"Oh yes. Run out front. When they arrive, sneak them in the side door and then upstairs to the ballroom." She glares at me, confused. "Why are you still standing here? Hurry." She shoos me out.

I rush out to the front of the conservatory and peer down the long driveway at all the cars arriving, excited teenagers and kids piling out of them. After a few minutes, a white SUV pulls into the circle, and Mila and Dylan step out.

"Thanks, Uncle Joe. We'll call you when we need to be picked up," Mila says before shutting her door. She waves as the SUV circles and exits down the drive, then heads over to me in her short swirly dress. An elastic wrap covers her ankle, but she shows no signs of limping.

Dylan swaggers behind her, staring at his cell. He's wearing his signature beanie, tight jeans, and white t-shirt.

A t-shirt? For Alison's sixteenth birthday? I bet that's the same one he slept in.

"Jeez," he says to Mila, "this place is in the middle of nowhere." He then turns to me. "What's up?"

Neither of them is carrying a present. I'm hoping Dylan has a jewelry box in his pocket. If not, I'm going to be in big trouble for breaking that music box.

"So what's the plan here?" Mila asks me.

I explain everything as I take them to the side door and then to the ballroom. It's packed with students and their guests. By now, they all know this is not just an open house, but also a surprise party. A banner draped across the entry says *Happy Sweet Sixteen, Alison.* From the high ceiling, a vintage disco ball casts colored fragments of light across the ballroom. At the far end, perched between balloons and flowers, a towering cake sits on a pedestal.

"Wait by these doors so Alison can see you when she comes in," I direct Mila and Dylan. Then I head to the cake for a better look.

"I hope Alison likes it," Louise says, appearing beside it. "See those pointe shoes and flowers on the sides of the layers? I made them with pink icing. Everything's edible except for the ballerina figure on top. It's Madame's—she let us borrow it."

"That's the most beautiful cake ever." I give Louise a big hug. "Alison will love it."

"Thank you, honey. Wait until you taste it. The best part is the filling—chocolate and vanilla mousse with strawberries."

"That's sounds super delicious, but it's too pretty to eat."

"Even beautiful things come to their end. Like myself." Louise cackles. "Can you believe I was once a looker? I had three young men chasing me when I was a little older than Alison."

Madame Dupree enters, clapping her hands. "Quiet everyone, please. Miss Natalia will bring Alison here in a moment." She points to me. "Kiki, please bring Alison's friends right in front."

As we gather round, Dylan whispers to me, "So, how long is this party anyway?"

"Get ready," Madame Dupree says.

The door opens and Alison walks in. Everyone shrieks, "Surprise!"

Alison stands there dazed, and then her eyes flick around and widen as she takes in the banner, the cake, and her friends. Her hands fly to her mouth. "This is for me?"

I rush over and hug her. "Happy birthday. Sorry I had to fib."

Alison's teary eyes glisten. "I had no clue." She throws her arms around Dylan. "I can't believe you're here. I'm so happy."

"Yeah, it was a long trip," he says.

"And Mila," Alison says, kissing her on the cheek. "Thanks so much for coming."

"Interesting dress." Mila says to Alison. "Is it new or old? I can never tell with those boho ones. That chiffon scarf is kind of pretty though." She then points to me and laughs. "At least you grew out of your polka dot phase."

I feel my face redden.

"I think Kiki looks adorable." Alison wraps an arm around my shoulder.

"You know I was only kidding," Mila says, nudging me.

Electronic club music starts blasting from the speakers. Most of the students rush to the center and start dancing with their friends. It's strange seeing all the rigid ballet students letting loose, just freestyling.

"So, how are classes going?" Mila's face pinches as she peers at Alison.

"Great. I love it here, especially the teachers." Alison's smile fades after she glances at Mila's ankle. "I'm really sorry you got hurt and couldn't come."

"So is my mother," Mila says, her voice tight as a knot. "She's furious with me."

"For spraining your ankle?" I ask.

"For anything that gets in the way of precious ballet. All I did was play a little soccer." A deep frown creases her forehead. "Heaven forbid I try to have a little fun."

"That's ridiculous," Dylan mutters.

"My dear sweet mother has my future all planned out. By the time I graduate in two years, she expects me to dance full time with a top ballet company." Mila glances down. "I was thinking about going to fashion design school. But when I told her, she went ballistic."

"Listen to me," Dylan says, finally looking up from his phone. "Do whatever you want. The heck with anybody else."

"Do you know how to sew?" I ask her.

"I made this dress." Mila twirls around. "What do you think?"

Alison leans in closer to examine it. "I love that turquoise color and all those crisscrossed ties in the back. I can't even sew a button."

"Thanks." Mila flicks her sleek black hair over her shoulder. "Hey, speaking about making stuff, did you hear about Dylan's painting?"

"Which one?" Alison asks.

"It's a new one." A proud smile tugs at his lips. "The Galaxy Coffee Shop bought it. They had an unveiling party for it." He becomes more animated than I've ever seen him. "It's hanging above the red sofa."

Alison jumps over and hugs him. "I'm so proud of you. I'm sorry I missed that."

"It was fun," Mila says. "We all shot confetti cans when they pulled the sheet off the canvas."

I've never seen any of his work, but Alison thinks he is some kind of art genius. "What's the painting of?" I ask.

"It's reminiscent of a mid-twentieth century modern," he says, eyes back on his phone. "It turned out really cool."

I tilt my head. "I have no idea what that is."

"Retro future," he says, half-paying attention. "Like the Jetsons' cartoon."

"Oh," I say. I still don't know what he's talking about.

"Kiki loves to draw ballerinas," Alison tells him. "She's getting really good now."

"That's nice," he says, his gaze wandering past me.

The music changes and Alison reaches out to Dylan. "I love this song. Want to dance?"

He twists his mouth. "Sorry, you know I hate dancing. No offense."

As Alison lowers her hand, Mila grabs it. "Come on, I'll dance with you."

Alison beams, then hesitates. "What about your ankle?"

"I can't go up on pointe, but I think I can handle this."

They head to the dance floor, and I'm left standing alone with her jerk of a boyfriend. I tell him I'm going to look for my friends and dart away, scanning the room for

Oliver. The blond boy is with the other two boys, but I still can't find Oliver.

"Great party," Darla says, popping up behind me. "Want to dance? Pretty please?"

"All right," I say. As soon as we get on the floor, she starts jumping around with her hands in the air like one of the Peanuts gang. When the song ends, I say I need a glass of punch and escape before the next song begins.

At the refreshment table, I bump into the blond boy, who is shoving potato chips in his mouth. I feel my face flush, but I ask anyway. "Have you seen Oliver?"

He smirks. "Sorry, Lover Boy couldn't make it. He's sick."

Before I can tell him off, he grabs two soda cans and runs off.

So that's why Oliver hasn't been around the last few days. Poor Oliver has to miss all of this—and the cake too. Maybe I can sneak to his cabin and bring him a slice. It stays light pretty late, and I think I remember how to get there.

I turn at a touch on my arm and find Suzie with a girl who she introduces as her cousin Emma. They insist I dance with them and drag me out to the floor. While I'm dancing, I catch sight of Adam and Clarissa standing by the ballroom entrance. I tell Suzie I'm going to get a drink and head toward them, hoping to hear what they're whispering about. But they leave before I can get close enough. Alison remains immersed with Mila and Dylan, so I leave her alone and hang out with Suzie and her cousin.

A ringing bell makes everyone quiet, and the music volume lowers. We all turn to Madame Dupree, who is standing by the cake. "Gather round everyone," she announces. As she lights each of the sixteen candles, the ballroom lights dim.

Alison heads over to the cake, her eyes shining in the glow of the candlelight. While we all belt out "Happy Birthday," I notice Dylan is not singing. I guess he's too cool for that. When Alison blows out the candles and makes a wish, I'm certain it involves him.

After Louise cuts the cake and hands out the slices, I consider asking her if I can bring one to Oliver. But I'm sure she'll say it's too late. So instead, I scarf mine down and ask for a second helping.

Louise grins. "You must really like it."

I nod.

"Well, there's plenty here." She cuts through one of the toe shoes and places the slice on a plastic plate. "Enjoy," she says as she hands me another napkin and fork.

I thank her, and as I walk away, I stick the fork in my pocket and place the napkin on top of the cake. While everyone is eating and pouring refreshments, I sneak out of the ballroom into the empty hall. After a quick look behind me confirming I'm alone, I hurry downstairs out the back door. Outside, the fresh mountain air fills my lungs. I glance up at the partygoers' silhouettes in the lit ballroom windows and then run to the path leading to the woods.

CHAPTER
EIGHTEEN

The Book with No Words

The deep violet sky above the forest is already fading to darkness—it's later than I thought. If I don't hurry, I'll never find my way to Oliver's cabin. With the plastic plate and cake in hand, I run between the hedgerow and through the pines. When I come upon the fairies' weeping willow, I halt and peek under the branches. It's dark, but someone has placed a tiny paper scroll under the tree. My pulse quickens as I untie the green ribbon and unroll the parchment paper. I carry it toward the lake, where the night sky reflects brighter.

This time, the warning is in English: *We've been more than patient. Where is our present?*

Present? That means the fairies never got my cookies. That black squirrel, Ziggy, must have stolen them. But it's too late to go back now and find something to give them. I rack my mind and then glance at the birthday cake I'm holding. But this slice is for Oliver. Then again, the fairies are so tiny, maybe an itty-bitty portion would be good enough.

I cut a piece of the cake with the fork and place it on the parchment, then set it under their tree, hoping that satisfies them. The last thing I need are more wasps—or any other painful pranks.

I glance around and catch pairs of silver eyes, blinking in the brush. "Are you the fairies—I mean, the good folk?" I ask, remembering what Oliver told me.

I wait, but the forest remains silent. "If you are watching me, please note this delicious piece of birthday cake I'm leaving under the tree. This should make us even. It's not my fault Ziggy stole the other present."

I place the napkin on Oliver's remaining portion, hoping the fairies won't mind that I kept the rest—or that Louise baked the cake and not me. I did bring it here myself, so that should count. As I continue toward the cabin, I pass Oliver's and Jeremiah's rowboats pulled up on the bank of the lake. An owl hoots in the distance, and another one answers. The violet-streaked sky has deepened to indigo. I hurry toward Oliver's cabin, using the rising moonlight to help guide me. When I get closer, an orange glow from the cabin windows leads me the rest of the way.

I bang on his door and wait.

A moment later, Oliver opens the door a crack. His eyes widen. "Kiki? What are you doing here?"

I wait for him to let me in, but he doesn't. "I came to—"

"Isn't tonight the open house party?"

"It's actually a surprise party for my sister. Sorry, I couldn't tell anyone."

"Really? I wish I could come." He still doesn't open the door any wider. "How old is she?"

"Sixteen." I hold out the cake. "I brought this for you. It's chocolate and vanilla mousse." His eyes light up as I hand it to him. I can tell he wants to eat it, but he stays in the doorway. "Aren't you going to let me in?"

"Did you ever get chicken pox—or the vaccination?" he asks nervously.

"Chicken pox?"

"Yeah. See?" He points to red blisters on his face and neck. "I have them all over. I got it from a kid in class."

"Yikes. I did see one of the other boys scratching the other day. I don't think I've ever had chicken pox."

"What about the vaccine?" He scratches his neck. "This is very contagious."

"I'm not sure. Maybe Alison would know."

"Then you can't come in," he says firmly.

"What about your grandad?" I ask.

"He had it when he was young. He's not here now anyway." Oliver glances up at the black sky. "It's late, you'd better go back. I'll get you a flashlight."

I wait by the door for a moment until he returns.

"Here," he says, wearing gloves. "I didn't want to touch it with my hands."

"Thanks." I linger a second. "Well, I hope you feel better soon." I flick on the flashlight and start down the path.

"Kiki?" Oliver calls out.

I glance back. "Yes?"

"Thanks for the cake. And... you look really pretty tonight."

I can't be certain, but I think I see him blush. "You're welcome." I grin as I hurry away.

A chill in the air rises from the mist, and I rub the goosebumps on my arms. Weaving through the tall trees, I come upon the weeping willow once again and shine the flashlight underneath. The scroll with the cake is gone. I bend closer and find twigs in its place.

They spell out *Very good cake.* Next to the twigs, I find a miniature book, about two inches long and wide. The cover has a painting of a red sun rising. But when I flip through the tiny pages, they're all blank. I glance at the cover again and notice the title is *The Book With No Words.* From inside, a tiny card falls out. It says, *Keep this book with you tonight.* On the back of the card, there's a poem:

Make no mistake
It's never too late

To free the mind's cage
Open any page
Toss salt of toad's tongue
With these words sung:
Red light, red light
Pierce the dark night

I notice a tiny satchel on the ground, the size of a thimble. It's labeled "Salt of Toad's Tongue." Of course, what else would it be? I stick the frog salt and book in my pocket. I'm afraid to offend the fairies in case they're watching. What's all this "Red light, red light, Pierce the dark night" stuff about anyway? Very strange. At least the fairies got the cake.

The sky is now a black velvet curtain with the full moon as a spotlight. Branches crack in the darkness, sending shivers through my bones. Who knows what kind of nighttime creatures lurk out here? I run as fast as I can the rest of the way back.

As I make my way through the hedgerow, I hear a couple laughing in the back garden of the conservatory. Maybe it's Adam and Clarissa. I don't want to get in trouble for sneaking into the forest at night, so I remain hidden, hoping they'll leave soon. I creep to the edge and peek out. It's not Adam and Clarissa. It's Dylan and Mila. *What!*

They've stopped laughing. Now they're kissing.

Kissing!

A wave of nausea overcomes me. I feel like retching. Do I confront them? But I'm just Alison's kid sister—it's not my place. But Alison needs to know. The truth will break that stupid spell he's had on her. She'll leave the jerk and go back to being my Before Dylan happy sister. I hesitate. Do I tell her now or later? If I tell her now, she can break it off with him while he's still here and not have to worry about it for the rest of camp. I take a determined breath. It will be for the best.

I don't want Dylan and Mila to see me, so I backtrack though the maze of hedges. With my heart racing, I run across the side yard into the conservatory. I bolt up to the second floor and sprint down the hall to the ballroom.

Inside, Alison is laughing with some dancers from her class. That means she doesn't know about Dylan and Mila yet. They're making a fool of her—and on her birthday, of all days.

I take a deep breath and head over to her.

"Where were you?" she asks with a gentle smile. "Madame Dupree came in here looking for you. I figured since you don't like parties, you went up to your room to draw or something."

"I have to talk to you," I say.

"What's up?"

"You've got to see something."

"Can it wait? My friends and I were just—"

I yank her arm. "Now."

"Okay, okay." Alison shrugs to her friends as I drag her to the window.

"You don't have to act so rude," she says. "What's the matter with—"

"Look outside."

She leans towards the glass and narrows her eyes. "What am I looking for?" A second later, her mouth falls open. The color drains from her face and she steps back, slowly shaking her head.

A hand with two gold rings latches on my elbow, and I spin around. Clarissa's face looms over me. "Please come with me," she demands. "I need to talk to you about Madame Dupree."

I turn back to Alison, who's still staring out the window. She doesn't even notice Clarissa. I pull at Clarissa's hold on me. "But my sis—"

"It's important." Clarissa guides me forcefully out of the ballroom and down to Madame Dupree's office. "Please sit." She points to a chair in the empty room.

"I can't stay now, my sister—"

Clarissa presses her hand on my shoulder and I sit down. She smiles her too-bright smile. "In a minute. First of all, where were you?' She aims her phone at me. "And speak loudly."

I swallow. Is she recording me? "Am I in trouble?"

"Madame was very worried." Clarissa's tone reeks of fake concern. "She went to the ballroom looking for you, but no one knew where you were. Were you out in the woods? And don't lie."

"I went to bring cake to Oliver. He lives in a cabin in the woods with his grandfather."

"This late? All by yourself?"

I nod.

"And did you get captured by any ghosts?" Clarissa smirks.

I shake my head.

"So that's a no? Is that correct?"

"Yes. I mean no, I mean—"

"And did you come upon any fairies?" She snickers.

"I didn't actually see—"

"So that's another no. Good."

"Where is Madame Dupree now?" I ask.

"She's resting." Clarissa pauses a moment, her face flushed. "Is it hot in here?" She fans herself and then places the back of her hand on her forehead.

"Please, I have to go," I beg.

"All right, I have what I need." She shoos me out without a second glance.

I run from the office to the back door and peek outside. No one is in the garden now. I bolt upstairs to the ballroom. The party has broken up with only a few people still lingering. I ask if anyone has seen Alison, but no one has.

Great. Just great.

I run down the long hall, through the western wing, and straight to room twenty-seven. I bang on Alison's door. She's not there, but her roommate says her friend in the turquoise dress came in and took Alison's dance bag a while ago. I rush back down and check all the main rooms and studios on the first floor. No Alison. Some of the remaining guests are exiting the front doors, and I follow them out.

I immediately spot Dylan and Mila heading to her uncle's white SUV.

"Wait," I yell, running toward them.

Dylan gives a quick nod and climbs in the back seat. Mila turns to me.

"Where is she?" I shout.

A sudden wind tangles Mia's black hair across her face, and she brushes a leaf out of it. "Who?" she asks.

"My sister," I shout.

"I think she went for a walk in the woods."

"The woods?"

"Mila," her uncle yells from inside the SUV. "We gotta go. We're blocking the driveway."

Mila opens the car door and shrugs. "Maybe she just needed some air."

"But she doesn't know about the—" I catch myself before mentioning the Wilis. "It's dangerous at night."

Mila steps away from the SUV and looks straight at me. "I know," she says. "But I'm sure Alison's fine."

Mila knows? Knows what? That the woods are dangerous? Or that the Wilis wait for girls with broken hearts?

Before I get a chance to ask, the car behind their SUV beeps.

"Mila," her uncle yells again.

"Don't worry, she's probably back in her room by now." Mila climbs in the car and slams the door shut.

"How could you do this?" I screech through my tightened throat. "You were her best friend."

But Mila doesn't look at me, and Dylan's head is down with his earphones on. He yawns as the SUV pulls away.

I remain standing on the curb, stomach churning, blood rushing to my head. I hate them. And I hate myself. Why did I let Alison see Mila and Dylan kissing? I'm so stupid. I've got to find her.

CHAPTER NINETEEN

The Queen of the Sylphs

A cold wind curls around me as I run to the back garden and into the woods. Deeper into the forest, the conservatory's warm amber lights fade away. I must have left Oliver's flashlight at the school somewhere, and now my only guide is the misty moonlight filtering through the dark trees. I glance up at a ghostly haze circling the full moon. A horrifying image of the Wilis rising from their graves flashes in my mind. Alison is out there, lost and heartbroken. I've got to find her before they do.

I race as fast as I can to the lake, ignoring the thorns scratching my legs and tearing at my new polka-dot dress. My shouts into the dark for Alison remain unanswered. When I reach the weeping willow tree, I pause, gasping for air. I have no idea what time it is, except that it's very late. All the while, my mind keeps attacking me. I ruined Alison's party. It's all my fault for inviting Mila and Dylan. And it's my fault for telling Alison about the kiss. I thought she would just break up with him. I never imagined she would run off like this.

When I reach the lake's edge, my heart clenches. Alison's ripped scarf hangs from a thorn bush. Jeremiah's brown rowboat is still docked, but Oliver's red one is missing. Oliver's home sick—he couldn't have taken it anywhere. It had to be Alison. But why would she row across the lake at night?

At that moment, chimes ring in the distance. *Bong, bong, bong...* I count each one, all the way up to twelve— then silence. I gasp.

Midnight.

I've got to row across the lake and save Alison. I shove Jeremiah's boat into the water, climb in, and push off with an oar. Using all my strength, I row as hard as I can. But the boat turns in a slow circle.

"Come on," I yell to myself. "Get it together."

I force my weak left arm to match my right arm's strength, but it still takes forever to make progress across the black water. As I get closer, I head into a lilting breeze that carries a haunting melody. A distant cello moans, a sound that holds all the darkness and sadness that has ever tormented this world. Then violins and harps join in, their notes rippling across the water.

My boat bumps with a loud thump against something hard, and I almost leap to my feet. I look back and see that I'm just a few feet from the opposite bank. My boat has hit the red rowboat—the one Alison must have taken. It's drifted a few feet away from the shore. I jump out, the water knee-deep, and try to pull my boat inland. It's much heavier than I imagined, and it takes several good heaves and bracing my feet in the sand before it's secure. Oliver made it look so easy. Why did he have to get sick now? The last thing I need is for both boats to slip into the dark water and leave us stranded. Alison's boat has drifted farther out, as if being pushed by a ghostly hand to the other side.

As I head into the forest, a shrill wind rips through the gnarled trees. I rub the chill from my arms and hurry toward the music. The sad minor key notes turn sinister, and I run faster, my feet sinking into moss, spongy from the damp night. Trees crack and bend in the blackness. Slivers of cobwebs cling to my face and body. All around, the forest breathes in heavy gusts of wind.

A dense mist surrounds me and whispers, *"Come and dance…"*

My heart pounds against my ribs and my breath quickens with fear. But I can't turn back. I race deeper through the eerie moon shadows in the woods. My legs stumble on raised roots and jagged fallen branches.

And then I see it—the silhouette of the Tree of Decayed Dreams. It stands alone in the forest, as if all the other trees fear it. Panting, I halt when I reach it. Black limbs of death twist and curl out to me, beckoning. My neck and scalp prickle at the sight of it. The rotting black slippers of the dead dangling from every twisted branch sway in the night breeze. With every shiver of wind, I can almost hear the soft cries of the brokenhearted.

But something is different on the tree. Fear twitches through my whole body. Hanging from a low spindly branch, a pair of new pink slippers sways in the wind. With chills running through me, I step closer and see Alison's initials inside the shoes. How did they even get here?

Then it hits me. Mila jealous of Alison's star role in the spring ballet. Mila kissing Dylan. Alison's roommate saying Mila got Alison's dance bag from her room. She's gone to this school before, plus her family has a ski lodge in the next town. Maybe she knows about the curse of the brokenhearted. What if she wanted Alison out of the way? I'm such an idiot. Did I lead Alison straight into Mila's trap?

I can't leave Alison's slippers here, a symbol that she's already joined the Wilis. I try to snatch them from the tree, but the slippers' ribbons tangle on thorns. Frantic, I clutch and pull at the ribbons, twisting them one way, then the other. The thorns cut my fingers, drawing drops of blood. I rub my hands on my dress—anything not to stain the slippers.

With a deep breath, I slow down and methodically remove each thorn from its hold on the ribbons. Just as I free the last one, a big gust of wind knocks me to the ground as something massive swoops from above and lands on the tree. I fall hard on my back, the pointe shoes in my hand. I blink and look up at the dark shape of the creature.

Purple talons from its three legs grip a thick twisted branch. Its grey-feathered chest swells as it takes in a big breath, thrashing enormous grey wings. I look away before I make eye contact with it—I don't want to see the blood-red eyes Oliver warned me about.

It's a rat-grey slawk.

I take off running. A shrill screech echoes behind me and then gets closer. When I can feel the air from its wing-beats, I throw myself to the ground. The three legs graze my back, snagging my dress but not latching onto me.

As soon as the slawk soars up, I leap to my feet. Running between trees with the rat-grey creature circling above, I pause to grab two large rocks. The first one I hurl at the slawk misses. My next shot hits it square on the chest, but that only angers it more. The monster bird squawks again. This time, shock waves of explosive lightning shoot from its red eyes.

I shriek and duck. The white-hot bolt passes inches above my head and strikes a tree, slicing it in half. Seconds later, the beast plunges again, heading between the trees toward me. The bird's too fast to outrun. I drop to the ground.

I'm thinking how doomed I am when a nightmarish roar from another creature fills the forest. The slawk turns its head and misses the opening between the pines. It smacks into a tree and falls to the ground. I can't tell if it's dead or only knocked out. Either way, it's my chance to escape.

As I jump up, the other animal's glowing eyes glare at me from the forest. The creature grumble-snorts as its rippling muscular limbs creep toward me. My body gears up to run. But I'm trapped between a thicket of brambles and the huge slawk lying in front of me.

As the animal gets closer, I make out its black glossy fur and gaping jaw, filled with razor-sharp teeth—ready to bite. It looks like a black jaguar. What the heck is a jaguar doing in these woods? Blood rushes through my veins. The jaguar creeps around the slawk's body and stops a few feet in front of me. Its long pink tongue licks its white teeth. I brace myself against a tree, my heart thudding violently. In a second, I'll be dinner.

But the black jaguar halts. It shakes its body like a wet dog, and as it shakes, its body shrinks, shapeshifting to the size of a house cat. I gasp as the cat stares up at me. One eye is amber and one indigo.

Can't be.

The cat meows and saunters closer to me.

I feel my own eyes widen to the size of saucers. "Koshka?" I say, not fully believing any of this.

The black scrappy cat purrs softly.

My mouth drops open. "You're a jaguar? I don't understand." But then again, there wasn't much about these woods that I did understand.

Koshka rubs against my leg and purrs even louder.

I pet the top of his head. "How did you do that? And how did you even get here?"

Koshka lingers a moment, and then slinks off. He disappears before I get a chance to thank him. But I have no time to find him now. I hurry toward the music with Alison's slippers slung across my shoulder. As I pass the iron gates to the graveyard, a figure appears in the mist. It soon takes form as a ghostly woman with airy wings in a long wispy tutu and white veil. She looks like she stepped out of Madame Dupree's ballet book. My bones shiver as I hide behind the trees. I blink, hoping I'm imagining it.

Her face isn't clear behind the veil, but her breathy voice floats in the air. "Who... are... you?"

My throat tightens. I can't speak. I'm frozen in place.

"Who... are... you?" The voice grows louder, demanding. "Speak."

"Kiki," I say around a tight ball in my throat. "I'm looking for my sister."

The ghostly woman moves toward me. "Your sister is where she belongs now. Soon, she will no longer be part of your world."

"No," I shout. "You can't have her. She's only sixteen."

"Many here are that age." She gestures toward the graves. "And we never grow any older."

My body trembles. "Please, tell me where she is."

The ghost sylph laughs, a horrible grating sound. "You're too late. The queen of the Wilis has risen from her grave. She will never allow your sister to leave."

"No," I scream, and dodge around the sylph to run toward the airy music floating through the trees. Ahead, a mound rises in a clearing, and dozens of ghostly ballerinas with white gossamer wings dance in a circle on top of it. Dressed in white flowy gowns and sheer veils, they look like brides. But there are no grooms here. Dreamlike, the full moon casts a blue light upon them. Cold sweat drips down my back as I crouch behind a thick bush. The music turns somber, and the ballerinas rise on white pointe shoes.

While the sylphs *bourrée* with tiny steps, their graceful arms flutter with sadness. Slowly, the Wilis glide back, revealing a solitary figure standing in the middle of the knoll. I gasp. It's Alison. She's still in her flowery party dress, but it's stained and shredded. Barefoot, she sways, her eyes half closed.

My mind races. Do I run out and grab her? Do I have time to get Jeremiah or someone else? Something icy cold touches my shoulder, but I'm too focused on Alison to really notice.

"Let Alison be." The sinister voice surrounds me, deeper and louder than the one before.

I leap up with a startled shriek. A shimmery winged sylph holding a silver scepter floats behind me. A chill shoots down my spine. Through her veil, I recognize the ice-blond curly hair from Madame Dupree's old photo. Priscilla, dead almost a hundred years. My shriek morphs into a scream that pierces the woods.

"Alison belongs with the Wilis now," the ghost of Priscilla says. "She is better off with us. Your world brings only heartache."

"No," I yell. "She belongs with my dad and me."

"Her heart is already broken. There is no turning back now."

She turns from me and vanishes, then reappears on the mound next to Alison. Priscilla waves her scepter at the Wilis, and they dance around Alison, weaving intricate patterns. Soon, Alison is dancing too, and as the hypnotic music grows louder and the tempo increases, she twirls faster and faster. Her turns and steps build to a frenzied madness.

If the legends are true, Alison will become a Wili for eternity if she remains in the circle and dances until dawn. I must stop her. But how? Do I run back, call Dylan, and beg him to save her? He would never believe any of this. And even if he did come, and he told Alison he still cared for her and was sorry, she would know he was lying.

Alison has a broken heart. What can fix that? My mind latches onto one idea. I don't know if it will work, but it's the only chance my sister has. I have to get close enough to talk to her.

With my heart hammering, I run toward Alison. As I get closer, the suffocating scent of death nauseates me. I hold my breath and push through, gagging on the stench. Ghostly spirits surround me. From beneath their veils, they glare into my soul with their dead eyes. I shriek out for Alison, but she keeps dancing, oblivious of me. I try to push forward, but the Wilis close in, dancing around me in circles. The forest blurs, their spinning casting some kind of spell. My stomach lurches and my legs weaken. I fall to my knees.

The day Mom died surges through me. After her sickness ripped her away, the heart of our home stopped beating. People said it would get better in time. Dad tried, but the black hole that took her place remained. We all just walked around it.

That familiar darkness approaches again, threatening to overcome me. I haven't lost my sister yet. I can't give up on her. I breathe deeply, fighting the urge to faint. I have to keep it together, for her, me, and my dad. I have to save her. The Wilis swirl around, blocking me.

"Such an annoying little thing." Priscilla sneers at me from her position on top of the mound. She points her scepter at me. "Enough of you, child."

A current of black wind blasts in my direction, but instead of knocking me back when it reaches me, it seems to absorb into my skin. Blood rushes to my brain, and my vision tunnels. *Don't faint... don't faint...*

The next time I open my eyes, I'm surrounded by darkness. Something silky is hanging around my shoulders—Alison's slippers. But I'm not on the knoll by Alison and the Wilis anymore. Where am I?

I blink and feel around me, waiting for my eyes to adjust to the moonlight. I'm in a dark, narrow place made of… dirt. Dirt? I gasp. I'm in a hole. A deep dirt hole in the shape of… no, no, no. Anything but this.

I'm in a hole the shape of a grave.

But I'm alive. I know that. My leg prickles as an insect scurries across it. Yeech. This isn't some horrible nightmare—Priscilla must have placed me in this grave. But how long have I been down here? *Oh no.* What about Alison?

The night sky above is still black. That means Alison could still be alive. I have to save her. But how do I get out of this grave?

I stand and claw at the dirt walls, trying to climb. The dirt crumbles in my hands, showering my head and forcing me to close my eyes. The top is still a couple feet above my outstretched arms. Blood throbs in my ears. I can't breathe. *Don't panic,* I tell myself over and over. I dig deeper into the dirt walls with my hands, desperate, clawing like a dog.

My hands hit something harder in the dirt wall, and as I dig around it, I realize it's a tree root. As I pull against it, it doesn't give, so I kick out places for my feet in the wall and hoist myself a foot higher. Then I continue to dig with my left hand as my right hand clings to the root. I fall back to the grave floor a couple times to give my exhausted arms and shoulders a break, but I only allow a brief rest before I climb back up and keep digging—and find another root. This one is thinner, more bendy, but I grab onto it and begin kicking into the wall to create a foothold. But what's that hissing sound behind me?

Oh no. Please not a snake! I glance down to see something writhing in the dirt. I start shaking and gasping for air. I have to get out. The thin root starts to give, but with one last pull, I heave myself up and crawl out.

Over my heavy breathing, the ghost music continues to envelop the forest. The darkness means I still have a chance to free Alison. Clambering to my feet, I brush off the dirt and mud covering my body. I glance at the Wilis' headstones surrounding me and remember my plan. Fake love caused all this. Maybe real love can save her.

My heart thumping, I run back to the tree of rotting slippers, Alison's pink ones bouncing against my back with each step. I grab a pair of black slippers, the laces slimy in my hand, and race back to the mound. Alison is there, dancing in the circle of the Wilis. Behind her, the sky is getting lighter, silhouetting the treetops at the edge of the clearing. Dawn is coming.

I take a deep breath. *Do it... now.*

Using all my will power, I barge through the circle of unsuspecting Wilis and run to Alison. "You can't leave me," I cry. "Dylan and Mila are not worth this."

Alison pauses and gazes at me with cloudy eyes.

"How did you get out?" Priscilla shouts, then commands in a booming voice to Alison, "Keep dancing."

Alison sways, her face pale from exhaustion.

"Faster," Priscilla demands.

Alison's knees buckle but she remains upright. Somehow I know that if she falls, I'll lose her forever.

I raise the black slippers, trying to get her to focus on me. "Is this what you want? Eternal death?"

Alison stares at me, confused.

"I know Dylan's love was a lie. But what about Dad and me? We both love you—and that's real." I choke back the tears. "You can't give up. I need my big sister back."

Priscilla's shrill laugh pierces my ears. "A family's love isn't enough—theirs is a love of obligation. Only the romantic love of your true soulmate makes life worth living. But such love does not exist." Hate fills every word, and she waves her scepter, swirling up a fierce wind that howls through the forest. A dense black fog rises from the ground as the music reaches a deafening crescendo. The other ghosts wail their agreement, and Alison begins to dance again.

"Alison," I shriek. "If you choose hate, that's where you'll end up forever." I point to the tangled graveyard.

Alison pauses, her gaze on the cemetery. "Where am I?" she asks, her voice barely a whisper.

"Love is waiting for you—right here." I drop the black slippers and reach my hand to her.

Her eyes blink, and she stares as if seeing me for the first time tonight. "Squeak?"

"Yes, it's me." Tears fall from my eyes.

She reaches out and stumbles toward me. "I don't feel well."

I grab Alison's hand and yank her away from the mound.

"Release her!" Priscilla shakes her scepter and a thunderclap explodes in the sky.

"Run, Alison." I tear off, pulling her with me.

CHAPTER TWENTY

Of Red Dragons and White Eagles

The Wilis howl and surge forward. Gasping, I tighten my grip on Alison, pulling her past reaching tree limbs, their branches snapping against us. Alison stumbles on a root, and as I turn to steady her, the Wilis swirl into a death circle, trapping us at the center.

Priscilla rips off her veil and reveals her rotted face. "Pretty—isn't it? And now it's your turn." She points to Alison.

"No," I shriek, jumping between her and Alison. "You can't take her future away. She's going to be a prima ballerina!"

"You insolent child! You think our futures were not promising?"

I swallow hard. "I... I didn't mean—"

"We all had our lives ahead of us." Priscilla motions to the other Wilis. "We made one fatal mistake—we let another take our power away. But enough regrets." She glances toward the empty grave. "It's time. We must have her before first light."

"No," I cry. "Take me instead."

"Don't try to bargain with me," Priscilla bellows. "Perhaps we will take you in a few years. But it is too late to save your sister."

Her words remind me of the fairies' poem: *It's never too late.* Something small heats up in my pocket. It's the tiny book. I yank it out and the pages flip open. As the sylphs close in, I sprinkle the toad salt on the page. I'm supposed to sing... something about light?

As the Wilis' ghostly arms grab for us, Alison cries, "I'm so sorry."

The words of the poem come back to me—at least some of them. "Red light, red light," I sing at the top of my lungs. "Pierce the dark night."

The book flies out of my hands, landing open on the ground. Pages begin turning as if the book is flipping through itself, searching. Then the flipping stops and a flicker of a flame rises from the chosen page. We all peer down, even the Wilis, as a symbol of the sun burns into the page. The fire swells, hissing and crackling with sparks, until it suddenly shoots up as a bolt of burning red light, soaring into the night. The Wilis freeze. A second later, an orange-red glow from the rising sun cuts through the trees.

Priscilla glares at the first ray of light and shrieks, "No, no, no! It's two minutes early!" She points to me. "You'll pay for this." With her fist to the sky, she wails, "I, who am of the air but doomed to dwell deep in the earth, call upon the winds of the darkest of ghouls. Curse these two and their school." Her ghostly form shudders and jerks as waves of spasms overtake her.

Alison and I remain transfixed as all the Wilis writhe in agony. Their bodies wither and slowly fade into a mist that floats over to the cemetery. As they sink into the mangled graves, I glare at the cemetery and then to the horizon. Did the sun really rise sooner? I think of Jeremiah's lab and the mysterious symbols. Was this alchemy? I peer back at the book, which is now burning to ashes.

"Is it over?" Alison asks, still in a daze.

I wrap my shaking arms around her. "You're safe now," I say. But are we? What was that curse about us and the school? I grab Alison's hand. "Hurry, we've got to go."

After we run a short distance, she halts and leans her hand on a tree trunk. "My feet hurt."

"The Wilis cast a spell on you. They forced you to dance all night. But you can rest when we get back." I grab her arm again, but she doesn't budge. She's staring at her feet.

Even in the dim light, I can see the tips of her toes are turning blue. My stomach clenches at the sight of them. I don't know how to tell her what's happening, so all I say is, "We have to hurry—before it's too late."

I pull her with me, her arm now ice-cold, and she limps as fast as she can. A high-pitched wind follows us as we rush through the forest. Soon the wind grows into an angry wail. When we finally reach the shoreline, Alison rests for a moment. The blue color has spread to the top of her toenails.

The red boat Alison rowed here has drifted toward the other side of the lake, but the brown one I used is still on the shore. After I help Alison into the boat, I shove it deeper into the water and climb in. I drape Alison's slippers around her neck, and since she's weak and shivering, I do all the rowing. The howling wind follows us, churning the water into angry waves. It still feels weird to row backwards, but a rush of adrenaline pumps through me, filling me with added strength.

"Look," Alison says, her voice faint. She points toward the water behind me.

In the distance, spindly sticks poke up from the middle of the lake. As I row closer and glance back again, I gasp. These are not twigs. They're bony fingers attached to arms rising from the depths. My heart stops. With a great splash, several decomposed faces bob to the surface. I shriek. The faces and skeletal arms move through the water and grab onto our boat.

"Save us," they moan.

Fear prickles my scalp. I know who they are. They're the men the Wilis drowned. "Get away," I shriek, smacking the closest down with an oar. "Alison, take this—" But Alison is slumped over, her eyes closed.

I drop the oar and shake her. "Wake up," I yell. Her chest gently rises and falls, but she remains in a deep sleep.

More bony hands circle, and the boat rocks hard enough that I drop the oars and clutch at the sides. "Someone help!" I scream. The thrashing grows more violent, and I'm terrified the boat will capsize.

"Save us," they hiss.

"You're dead," I shriek. "I can't save you."

"Save us or die." They pound on the boat, rocking it harder.

In the distance, a scratchy voice yells, "Kiki, hang on. I'm coming."

Oliver.

A moment later, he emerges from the forest across the lake. Wearing a football helmet and winter gloves, he races to the shore.

"Oliver, help," I shriek.

"I'm coming." He wades to the other floating boat, grabs the edge, and hoists himself inside.

While he rows with all his strength toward me, the ghouls continue battering my boat, and a crack appears in one side. Water starts seeping in. I kneel to balance myself and pick up an oar to bat at them. But there are too many, and soon another crack appears. "Hurry," I scream. "My boat's leaking."

By the time Oliver reaches me, my knees are submerged. He rows alongside, grabs hold of my boat, and yells, "Climb over to mine."

I shake Alison and yell, "Wake up." Nothing.

Oliver leans over to my boat. "We'll move her together." While he grabs her shoulders, I push her legs, and she slithers across into his boat, falling to the bottom.

"You next," Oliver yells. As I reach one leg across into his boat, the ghouls moan loudly and thrash. My boat shudders and flips, sending me into the slimy lake. Something claws at my ankle, then latches onto it. I'm pulled deeper, my head sinking below the lake. I can't breathe, and my eyes stare up through the water to the receding surface. A hideous ghoul swims above me, glaring down. Moldy shredded clothes from another century hang from its bones.

Oliver's screams of "Let her go" are muffled by the water.

His oar pounds the ghoul above me, sending him spinning away. With the last of my air and energy, I struggle against the ghoul at my ankle, kicking down hard with my other foot. As soon as the bony hand releases me, I burst to the surface, gulping for air. Oliver yanks me up into his boat and I flop inside next to Alison. But there's no time for rest. He hands me one oar to fend off the ghouls while he rows with the other oar.

By the time we reach the other side of the lake, we're both drenched and out of breath. We drag Alison from the boat, and as we rest her against a tree by the shore, her eyes open a slit.

"My feet," she whimpers. "They're so cold."

Oliver and I stare at her toes. They've turned completely blue.

"What's happening to them?" she asks, her voice weak. "Why are..." Her eyes close and she drifts into a sleep.

Oliver and I share a horrified look. "She needs those gemstones," he says, pointing to his cabin. "And we have to soak her feet in the lake."

Even though I doubted their powers before, I'll try anything. "Hurry and get them. I'll stay here with her."

"But I don't know which crystals are which," he says with a panicked look.

"What are you talking about? I thought you knew all this magic stuff."

"Not yet. It's not like Grandad labeled them, and he's not home now."

"Which ones are they again?"

"Rose quartz and yellow citrine."

"I know those ones. I'll go," I say in a rush.

"They're in tall wooden bowls. I think by the back wall."

I'm running before he's done talking, grateful at least that it's getting lighter so I can see my way. When I reach Oliver's cabin, I throw open the human-sized door and rush to the secret foyer. After placing my hand on the bronze skull, it seems to rotate in slow motion.

"Turn!" I yell.

The clunking starts, along with the *click, click, click,* and the paneled wall creaks open. I rush down the winding stairs, push open the heavy iron door, and race past the huge furnace to the back wall.

But there are no wooden bowls. I run around the lab, trying not to knock over anything. As I'm about to give up, a glistening behind a table holding a microscope and an antique balance scale catches my eye. I rush over, find the two bowls filled with crystals of all colors, and exhale with relief. But digging through them, I can't find the rose quartz and honey-colored citrine. Panicking, I dump all the crystals on the floor.

"Come on, come on," I say as I sift through the piles. Finally, I spot them. "Hallelujah!"

Crystals in my pocket, I rush outside, only to find the weather has gone horribly wrong. The red rising sun has vanished, and a murky darkness covers the sky. A moaning wind claws at me as I run, and my skin grows cold and clammy. Above the lake, black clouds churn, forming shapes of hideous creatures that seem to murmur and hiss with the wind. A ball of fear forms in my chest. Is this Priscilla's curse? Are these the winds of the darkest ghouls? Oh no. Please no. This can't be the end of us and the school.

The evil black mass in the sky looks so familiar. I've seen it before. But where? It wasn't a dream—it was something else. That picture I drew. From that painting in Jeremiah's gold book. It was all in there—even the alchemy symbols to fight it.

Maybe I can stop all this. But there's so little time. I'd have to decipher those symbols before this curse or whatever it is destroys everything. I start to run back toward the cabin, but then I think of Alison. If I don't get the crystals to her soon, she'll lose her toes. I scream for Oliver, but he's too far to hear me, especially over the roaring winds. Should I run to her and give Oliver the crystals and then run back here? But the weather is worsening by the second, and it won't do any good to save her feet if this curse destroys everyone.

"Please hang in there, Alison," I yell, even though I know she can't hear me, and I run back to the cabin.

Back in the lab, I find the gold-leafed book and riffle through the pages to the painting of the gruesome mist of swirling evil above a lake. The alchemists drew that white eagle and red dragon battling and devouring the curse. But where is that tiny droplet Oliver mentioned? I narrow my eyes searching the page. Then I see it—in the bottom right corner. But what is it? Oliver said they're all symbols for chemicals, but does Jeremiah even have them?

From outside comes a rumbling roar like a locomotive, rattling the cabin. The bubbling bottles clang against each other. Panting, I tear through the lab, peering at every bottle's label. I finally find one with a drawing of a white eagle and grab it. But where is the red dragon? I check the rest of the flasks and beakers on the shelves and counters with no luck.

As I start to lose hope, I spot a wooden case on a small table labeled HNO_3 along with a triangle symbol and a drawing of a red flame. *Could it be?* Breathless, I open the case, and there it is—a lidded glass cylinder with a small drawing of a red dragon. A combination of relief and fear comes over me as I carefully remove the bottle and head for the door. Then I remember that tiny drop on the painting. But Oliver said even Jeremiah didn't know what it meant. Which means it can't be here. I hope it's not too important.

I run outside, carrying the flasks into the swirling black winds. The gusts whip against my face as I race to Alison and Oliver. By the time I reach them, Oliver's already pulled her to the water's edge. She's lying on the bank with her feet submerged.

"Hurry," he shouts. "Her toes are turning black."

"Take the crystals from my pocket," I shout.

He eyes the flasks, then does as I say and places the citrine in Alison's right hand and the rose quartz in her left. As he closes her fingers around them, the monstrous mist twists and howls.

"How long does this take?" I shout, eyeing the seething, expanding black mass above our heads.

"You're asking me?" Oliver says, his voice shaking.

We both stare at her feet as fierce winds batter the forest. Slowly, the tops of Alison's toes transform from charcoal black to bruise blue. She moans in her sleep and wiggles them, and moments later, their fleshy-pink color returns.

"We did it," I yell.

A strong wind buffets me, and I almost spill the flasks. Black funnel clouds form in the sky, and I can hardly stand against the ferocious wind vacuum.

I stare at the flasks. "What should I do?" I shout.

"Pour them together," Oliver yells, kneeling on the ground shielding Alison to make sure the wind doesn't carry her off.

My heart pounds. What if these chemicals release an even greater evil? Or an explosion? No time to second guess now. I hold my breath and pour the contents of the red dragon flask into the white eagle one. Oliver and I glare at the sky and wait.

And we wait.

As we watch, the funnel clouds grow until they touch the surface of the lake, sucking up water and ghouls. The three of us will be next, and then Oliver's cabin, the school, and everyone in it. I drop the empty flask and help Oliver move Alison from the water's edge to a large nearby tree, sitting her against its trunk. Its branches rattle and shake, but I hope it is strong enough to keep standing. Behind us, the wind sucks Oliver's boat up into the funnel.

Still clinging to the full flask, I huddle under the tree next to Alison, who is slowly waking up. Oliver sits on her other side, and I check the flask again. Still nothing. All the trees around us are bending toward the funnel, and some start cracking, sending branches and leaves whirling past us. Cold sweat drips down my back. I try not to think about how in a moment, all three of us will be swirling in that blender of ghouls. Poor Dad will be heartbroken without us.

"I love you, Dad," I whisper. As I lower my head from the raging wind, a teardrop from my eye falls into the flask. I brace for the ripping wind.

Oliver is yelling something, and it takes a second for me to process what he's saying. The chemicals are starting to bubble?

Sure enough, inside the flask the liquid is boiling violently. I almost drop it.

"We have to leave Alison here and go out into the open," he yells, grabbing my hand. "Say something magical!"

"Magical?" I shout as we hurry out from under the tree. "What are you talking about?"

"Say anything!"

I glance from the flask to the oncoming funnel and back to the flask. I can't think of what to do. My mind is racing. Suddenly, I think of my mom. I think of her laugh and her smile and her polka-dot apron. "Lubbly jubbly!" comes bursting out of me.

The liquid gurgles more and Oliver waves me on with frantic hands. "Keep going. Rhyme something!"

"Lubbly jubbly. This stuff is bubbly." I'm grasping at straws.

"It's working! Say more stuff."

I holler, "No time to wait, let love melt hate!"

The chemicals erupt and the glass shatters in my hand. We both jump back as red and white vapors burst from the flask. They shoot into the sky like Roman candles. The red vapors twist and swirl into the shape of a massive horned dragon. Spiked scales appear down the length of its back and coiled tail. Huge bat-like wings emerge, spanning over a hundred feet. The dragon whirls through the black clouds, blasting a furnace of fire-red vapor from its nostrils and mouth. Hot winds roar and burn in the sky, the heat stinging our eyes.

While the red dragon's flames devour the ghouls and blackness, the white vapors form the shape of a colossal eagle. The phantom-white eagle glides to the tallest evergreen, which barely bends under its weight. Perched there, it waits while the gruesome black sky creatures moan and wail in misery from the dragon's fire. When the last of the blackness has burned, the noble eagle spreads its broad wings. It soars through the sky, blanketing the flames with cool vapors. The sky turns a blinding, blizzard-white, and for a moment, Priscilla and the Wilis appear, floating in the mist.

Then with a whoosh, everything is sucked down into the lake. For a minute, waves slosh the shore while the ground beneath us trembles, but then all stills. The sky clears to crystal blue, and the sun reappears in the horizon.

Oliver and I share a look of shocked relief. Still trembling, we hug each other. We made it.

"How did you know to come for us?" I ask, my voice still shaky.

"My bedroom window was open. I woke up when I heard your screams."

"Kiki?" Alison moans.

Oliver and I rush over, and she stares at him, rubbing her head. "Who are you? And why are you wearing a helmet and gloves?"

A smile crosses my lips. "This is Oliver."

He points between the metal bars to his face. "I've got chicken pox. I don't want you to catch it."

"We got shots years ago," Alison says, her voice weak. She stands, using the tree for support.

"That's good." He scratches his arms through his shirt.

Alison takes a step toward me and puts her hand on my shoulder, swaying. "Whoa, sorry. My balance is off. And I'm so tired…"

"I better get her back to rest. Are you coming?" I ask Oliver.

"Not till I'm all better."

"Well, I guess I'll see you then." I stand there a moment, trying to comprehend everything that's happened. "Thanks for—"

"I only helped," Oliver says. "You're the real hero here."

CHAPTER
TWENTY-ONE

Good Riddance

When Alison and I reach the conservatory, the halls are empty. I expected to see everyone running around like crazy after the insane storm. But the wall clock says it's only 6:28 a.m. Everyone must still be in bed. I'm surprised they slept through all that, but I'm also relieved the black storm didn't reach the school. If they had survived, it would have given the students nightmares for years.

I glance over at Alison, who is more herself but so tired she can barely stand. If I bring her to her room now, I might wake the others and cause a ruckus. Our torn clothes are drenched and filthy. I decide to look for Madame Dupree. She understands all this Wilis stuff, and since she's old, she's probably already in her office.

Madame's office door is open a crack. I tap on it and wait, feeling my own muscles' exhaustion. No one answers, so I peek in. Madame is not there, but since Alison is near collapse, I guide her inside, push some books from a chair, and help her sit down. After removing her slippers from her neck, I place them on her lap.

"Maybe Madame is in the kitchen eating breakfast," I tell Alison, who's already nodding off. "Rest here while I go check." I drape one of Madame's heavy, long scarves over her, then hurry out and close the door.

While rushing down the hall, I hear a muffled cry. I halt. I hear it again and trace it to the storage room. Who would be in there at this hour? I take a breath and twist the knob. It's locked. The person cries out again. I try again, but it's no use. Then I remember all the keys hanging in Madame's office.

"I'll be right back," I yell, and then race down the hall back to Madame's office.

Inside, Alison snores softly on the chair. I search through the keys, quietly at first until I realize Alison won't wake up to the jangling. I check all the hanging keys for the first floor—there must be at least thirty of them. No luck. Then I remember that Madame Dupree said she kept duplicates in her bottom desk drawer. I rush over, and after rummaging through the clump of keys for the first floor, I find one labeled *Storage Room*. I untangle it from the jumble of others and run down the hall.

When I reach the storage room, the person inside is still whimpering.

"I'm here," I shout, and slip the key in the lock. The key fits but won't turn.

The person inside cries again.

"It doesn't work," I say, jiggling the key. Then I try the method I use with my own house—slip the key in, pull it out slightly, and then turn it.

Voila! The storage door opens.

I gasp. It's Madame Dupree inside. Her mouth is duct-taped and her hands and legs are bound to a wooden chair with her own scarves. My heart beats out of my chest.

"Who did this to you?" I yell.

She whimpers through the tape.

"This is going to hurt," I say, remembering when my cousin duct-taped me once for a joke. "Ready?"

Madame nods.

"Here goes." I rip the tape from her mouth.

Madame cries in relief and then peers at me. "You look a fright. Your dress—it's all torn and wet. I was so worried about you and—oh no, please tell me your sister is—"

"We're okay," I say.

Suddenly, Adam appears in the doorway. "Oh my God. What happened?" He rushes over and helps untie her legs and hands. "A windstorm woke me up and I was heading to the kitchen—"

"Your precious Clarissa," Madame shrieks. "She did this to me!"

"What?" Adam's jaw drops.

"Your fiancée shackled me last night." Madame rubs the red bruised skin on her wrists.

Adams gapes at his aunt, his eyes bulging. "What are you talking about?"

"You heard me," she snaps.

Adam darts a confused look toward me. "Is that true?"

"I just got here. But if she says it's true, you should believe her."

Madame smiles at me. "Thank you, Kiki."

The veins in Adam's neck twitch. "Why on earth would Clarissa—"

"Because she's a horrible, horrible person." Madame winces and rises from the chair. "Last night during the party, I couldn't find Alison or Kiki. I wasn't sure if they would take Kiki, since she's younger, but I feared the worst for Alison."

Adam's eyes narrow. "Who are *they*? And what is *the worst*?"

"The Wilis," Madame yells. "I panicked. I tried to find you to help, but Clarissa grabbed me. She ordered me to be quiet and not act like a lunatic in front of everybody. She strong-armed me down here to talk in private. Once we were inside, she insisted on recording me while I told her about the Wilis. Then she tied me up and locked me in here."

"So that's why I couldn't find the key to this room," I say. "Clarissa must have stolen it from your office."

"Hold on." Adam makes a stop sign with his palm. "What on earth are the Wilis?"

Madame sighs. "They aren't of this earth. That's the whole point—they're ghosts."

I nod.

Adam's face turns pale and his eyes narrow at me. "You've seen them?"

"Yes," I say. "And they're horrible."

"Both of you, stay right here. I'm getting to the bottom of all this." Adam returns a few minutes later, dragging Clarissa in with him. Her flushed face is bare of makeup, her hair is a rat's nest, and she's dressed in a pink robe with only one slipper.

"What are you doing?" Clarissa shouts, pushing away from him.

"You!" Madame points to Clarissa. "How dare you hogtie me."

Clarissa smirks at Adam. "Your aunt really is out of her mind. I don't even have to make it up. Last night, she was ranting about ghosts in the woods—in front of everyone. The last thing we need is a lawsuit for running a school with an incompetent loon—the lawyers would clean out your whole inheritance. So I brought her here. And the great news is, I got it all on tape. I have enough to get her quietly committed. And once we get the money..." She trails off when she sees Adam's clenched jaw and furious eyes.

"How could you do this to my aunt?" His voice is quiet and dangerous.

"What are you talking about?" Clarissa looks at Adam wide-eyed. "I thought you wanted this. The life I deserve doesn't come cheap, you know."

"I never said I wanted any of this." He holds his head in his hands. "What was I thinking getting involved with someone like you. I can't believe I let you railroad your way into my life." Adam turns his back to Clarissa and faces his aunt. "I knew Clarissa could be shallow and greedy, but I never imagined she would go this far." His eyes tear up as he touches Madame's hand. "I'm so sorry."

Clarissa yanks Adam's hand away from Madame's. "What about—"

"What about nothing," Adam says, pushing Clarissa away. "I should never have let you anywhere near my dear aunt. I want you gone."

Clarissa opens her mouth to speak, but nothing comes out. A moment later, she starts scratching her neck and brushing herself with frantic jerky motions. "Bugs! Get them off me!"

I smile as I recognize the red welts forming on her skin.

"Why are you smiling?" Clarissa yells at me.

"You don't have any bugs on you," I say. "I guess you never had chicken pox before. Or the shot."

"Chicken pox?" She glares into a wall mirror and shrieks. "Oh my God. Sick kids, filthy woods, and your insane old aunt." She pulls Adam's arm. "Get me out of here. I've had enough of this horrid place."

Adam firmly removes his arm from her hold. "I'm staying right here." He gives Madame a searching glance. "That is—if I'm forgiven."

"Adam," Clarissa yells. "Carry my bags downstairs and pull the car around."

Adam ignores her.

"Adam," Clarissa whines, sidling up to him. "Please?"

"You'll have to get your own bags from now on," Adam says calmly, his attention still focused on Madame. "And call your own cab to the train."

Clarissa takes a step back like she's been slapped. "The train? I never ride on trains."

"You will now." A small grin quirks up the corners of Adam's lips, and Madame smiles at him.

Clarissa's mouth falls open. "But—"

"You heard me." He finally looks at her, his gaze steely as he points to the door. "And you've got five minutes to get off the property."

Clarissa scratches her neck and glares at him. "You're making a huge mistake."

"You're welcome to stay and explain that to the police," Adam says.

With that, Clarissa scampers away like a timid mouse, her one slipper flapping against the floor.

"Can you ever forgive me?" Adam asks Madame Dupree. "I promise I had no idea."

Madame studies him a moment and her eyes soften. "We'll talk about all this in private." She then turns to me. "Kiki, would you mind getting me a cup of tea from the kitchen—no milk, a bit of honey? We'll meet you in my office."

"Sure." I nod, then add, "My sister Alison is asleep in there—we were trying to find you..."

Madame Dupree waves a hand, looking relieved. "I'm just glad she's okay."

By the time I return from the kitchen, Adam and Madame are talking quietly in the office. From the tone of their voices, I know they've made up. I balance Madame's tea on top of a stack of books on her desk and she smiles her thanks. Alison remains sound asleep in the chair.

"Should I wake her and bring her upstairs, Madame?" I ask.

Madame looks at Alison and shakes her head. "She's been through quite an ordeal—one you'll have to tell me about. But later. Let her rest for now." Her wise gaze turns to me. "I expect you'd like to get cleaned up and take your own rest."

I nod, thank her, and leave, already looking forward to a warm shower. As I hurry down the hall, I almost run smack into a ladder. Jeremiah is balancing on top, polishing one of the huge wall clocks.

"Morning, Kiki," he says. "Sorry I couldn't be here last night—I just got back from taking care of other urgent matters. But I understand everything's under control now—thanks to you."

I shrug. "I just happened to find Madame."

His deep-set eyes bear into me, like he can see the events of the whole night play out in my mind. "Don't be so modest. I'm aware it was much more than that. I heard you had a terrible storm here." His voice lowers and he smiles. "Quite clever of you to figure out the missing ingredient."

I stare at him. "You know all about that?"

He nods as he straightens the clock.

"But I didn't really figure—"

"Ah, but you did with your love. The shedding of a single tear is more powerful than anyone can imagine."

For a second, I think of what could have happened, but then push it out of my mind. Everyone is safe now. I glance back up at Jeremiah and whisper, "Did you have to move the clock two minutes forward?"

He gives me a thoughtful knowing look. "No, my dear. The time is exactly as it should be. Sometimes the Earth's atmosphere affects the time we see the sunrise. It can refract or bend light in a way that makes the sun appear to rise earlier or later." He pauses a moment and rubs his chin. "I've heard a small book exists somewhere, capable of creating such an illusion." His eyes crinkle. "Perhaps you are aware of it."

I feel a smile tug at my lips. "Perhaps."

CHAPTER
TWENTY-TWO

Keeping the Secret

The next day, after a long sleep, Alison wakes up and seems to have her strength back. She remembers most of what happened, but some events remain fuzzy, especially toward the end. Madame Dupree, Adam, Oliver, Jeremiah, Alison, and I have a secret meeting. We all vow to keep that night a secret since no one wants the school to close.

Adam, fearing other students might venture across the lake, asks Jeremiah not to repair or replace the two boats, both of which were severely damaged in the storm. But Jeremiah tells him the Wilis are no longer a threat in these woods—the alchemy reversed the storm's power, turning their evil back on them and sealing them in their graves to finally rest in peace. Adam sighs with relief, as do the rest of us. Jeremiah continues to explain that he and Oliver still need the boats to look after additional otherworldly beings. When Adam's face turns pale, Jeremiah finishes by saying he will build a locked boathouse. This seems to satisfy Adam.

During the last week of dance classes, my concentration improves and I can see some progress with my turns. My technique still requires years of work, but at least it's a start.

With that blister of a boyfriend lanced from her life, Alison returns to her BD self—Before Dylan—but even better, with an extreme attitude improvement. The pointe shoes I snatched back from the Wilis get a workout from all her practicing, and it pays off. Her teachers say she dances with even more artistry than before, and they assign her the solo in her group's dance.

On the second to last day of camp, I catch sight of Oliver talking to his buddies in the hall. It's the first day he's been back since getting the chicken pox. When he notices me, he beams, and I rush over, even though I know it will embarrass him. I tell him we have so much to talk about and how much I missed him. He hugs me, and of course, his friends make comments. But this time, Oliver's fine with it.

During lunch, Alison and I get a few minutes to talk alone. She tells me Mila called.

I almost choke on my tuna sandwich. "Mila?"

"Yeah, I was shocked too. She said her jealousy got the best of her. She called to apologize."

"For trying to turn you into a ghost? I don't think there's a greeting card for that."

"Turns out, Mila didn't know anything about the Wilis. She did steal my slippers, but all she did was throw them in the woods."

"How can you be so sure? Did you ask her about the Wilis?"

Alison gives me an *of course not* look. "I couldn't— we're supposed to keep all that a secret. But I'm sure she was telling the truth. Plus, she and Dylan broke up anyway. She said the only person he cares about is himself."

I shake my head. "That part about Dylan sure is true, but I don't know about the rest of it. Are you still going to be friends?"

Alison pauses. "I'll have to see how it goes. But speaking of that night..." She takes hold of my hand. "I never thanked you for what you did for me." Her eyes go distant. "After I ran from the party, these weird blue lights made a path through the forest to my slippers. I remember picking them up and the lights leading me to the lake. It was like I had to follow them..." Alison stops and stares past me for a moment before squeezing my hand. "But so much of what happened is still fuzzy—like a horrible dream."

Blue lights? My breath catches. That means Will-o'–the-Wisps *were* outside her window that first night, waiting to lure her away.

She gives me a pained look. "I want to remember more, but I can't just yet."

I squeeze her hand back. "You're my sister, and I love you. That's all you need to remember." The image of Alison's broken music box flashes in my mind, and I wince. Alison looks at me curiously.

I take a deep breath. "I... have a confession to make." I explain everything about the brochure lights and her music box breaking the morning we left. "I'm really sorry," I finish. "I should have told you that morning."

She pauses, taking it all in. "Do you think that was some kind of omen?"

"I don't know. But maybe whatever happens is supposed to happen—the good and the bad."

"Sometimes you can be pretty wise, Squeak." Her eyebrows then draw together in a thoughtful frown. "But I do wish that music box wasn't broken."

I blink. "Why?"

A broad smile slowly spreads across her face. "I would have loved smashing it myself."

I grin back, relieved, then remember one other thing. "Oh, and when we get home, we might have to deal with a certain spider."

She gives me a questioning look before shrugging my comment away. "Talking about home, I spoke to Dad. He's coming tomorrow to watch us perform."

Thinking about him fills my heart with emotion. "I've missed him so much."

"Me too," she says softly. "But we can't tell him anything about—"

I nod. "Dad worries about us enough. He'd never let us out of sight if he knew."

"That's for sure," she says with a laugh. "Anyway, we weren't on long, it was a bad connection. But he said he loves us and can't wait to see our show."

I take a breath and bite my lip. Now I'm nercited again. But I'll just do my best. I realize that's all anyone can do.

CHAPTER
TWENTY-THREE

Places Everyone

The following afternoon, the students' parents start arriving for the presentation. Alison and I wait outside the conservatory to greet Dad when he pulls up. Nearby, Suzie and little Darla chatter away as they wait for their own families. Suzie spots her parents first and jumps up and waves at them. They rush out of their car and hug Suzie while her brother makes goofy faces at her. After Suzie introduces Alison and me to her family, they extend an open invitation to visit them in Orlando anytime we want.

Little Darla's family arrives next. Her three sisters, one older and two younger, bolt out of their SUV and run over to her. All the girls have the same popsicle-orange hair and bouncy personalities.

One by one, Alison and I watch the other students reunite with their families. I keep straining my neck, looking for Dad, but his green jeep never pulls up.

After an hour or so, when most families have gone inside, Alison lowers her head. "I guess he couldn't make it."

My stomach tightens. "You think everything's okay?"

Alison pulls out her cell. "There aren't any messages." She takes my hand. "Come on, we'd better go inside and get ready for the show."

Alison and I head back inside the conservatory, and as we make our way through the crowd of parents in the lobby, we hear, "There they are—my beautiful daughters."

We turn and see Dad rushing over. He's tanned and glows as if layers of sadness have peeled away. I guess doing what you're meant to do makes you shine from the inside.

"Sorry I'm late," he says, group hugging us. "I had to jump start the old jeep." He steps back and beams at us. "I've missed you two so much. We have tons to catch up on. But first, did you have fun here?"

"It wasn't boring," I say.

"*Definitely* not boring." Alison gives me a knowing glance.

The loudspeakers squeal, then Madame's voice comes through. "Last call. All students please report to the auditorium now."

"I'm so excited to watch your performance. Break a leg," Dad says, waving as Alison and I hurry off.

After we gather our costumes from the prop room, we run outside along the path to the theater's stage door. As soon as we enter the backstage area, we step into a swirl of buzzing energy. Everywhere we go, jittery students are making last minute hair and costume adjustments amidst panicky cries of *Oh no, I forgot the first step.* After we squeeze through the crush of girls in their puffy tutus, we rush to the dressing rooms. Alison's class has a separate room from the younger girls, so we each head our own way.

When I reach my room, I see that most of the students are already dressed. I fixed my hair in a bun earlier, but I still have to hurry and put on my costume and makeup. After I slip on my costume, I adjust the straps and study my reflection. I love the rose velvet bodice and long layered tutu shaded from light rose to dark. A smile springs to my mouth as I give the tutu a few puffs up and spin around. The costume is so pretty, I almost wish I could wear it all the time.

Miss Genevieve pops in to help me with my makeup, and I'm grateful for her assistance. She explained to us in an earlier class that without makeup, our faces get washed out onstage from the bright lights. After she sits me down, she applies foundation, a dash of blush, and pink lipstick. For my eyes, she uses light mocha eyeshadow with a flick of mascara, which looks perfect with my two different colored eyes. Before I rush out, she gives my hair a few spritzes of spray to hold it in place.

"Wait," she shouts as I head to the hall. "You forgot your headpiece." She grabs a flowered garland and secures it with bobby pins. "There," she says with an approving nod. "You look lovely."

"Thanks, Miss Genevieve." I hug her and rush to the hall. The first person I see is Oliver.

"Hurry," he says, and I follow him to the stage wings. He points to metal steps that lead to the catwalk. "Sit here. It's a great spot to watch the show."

"I thought performers aren't allowed in the stage area."

"They're not. But since I help Grandad with the lights and rigging, we can stay here."

"Oliver," Jeremiah calls. He's standing above on the catwalk, adjusting the hanging stage lights. "I need your help."

"Coming." Oliver bolts up the stairs. With a monkey's agility, he hangs from a rafter and fiddles with some wires.

I hold my breath, worried he might fall. A couple of minutes later, Oliver heads back down the stairs and sits next to me.

"Fixed it," he says, smiling. "By the way, you look awesome."

"Thanks. Your costume is cool too." He's wearing a pirate outfit with a headscarf, a white billowy shirt, and velvet dance pants.

"Coming through," Jeremiah says as he climbs down the steps. We nudge over. "I'm heading to the sound booth. Have a good show."

Groups of students are still milling around onstage, peeking out of the curtain to find their families, but Miss Sandy shoos them back to their dressing rooms. "Off you go. You too." She points to me.

I start to get up, but Oliver puts a hand on my arm. "She's helping me," he says.

"All right. But stay on the steps, out of the way. Remember, if you can see the audience, they can see you." She checks her watch. "We'll be starting in a minute or two."

A few moments later, Miss Sandy ushers onstage the students who perform in the opening dance. "Places, everyone," she says, and they all rush to their spots behind the closed curtain and whisper nervously.

The stage lights switch to a pink glow, and the low murmur from the audience quiets—Jeremiah must have dimmed the house lights. High heels click across the front of the curtain on the curved part of the stage called an apron. Oliver glances at me and grins. I try to smile back, but my stomach is fluttering away. The show's about to start.

CHAPTER TWENTY-FOUR

Lubbly Jubbly Everywhere

"Welcome, parents and friends, to our presentation," Madame Dupree announces over the microphone. "The students have worked very hard the last few weeks. I'm sure you'll be proud of them. So, without further ado, we shall begin."

The heavy blue curtain drags open across the stage and the music "Dance of the Hours" begins. I remain on the metal steps backstage and watch the first group. After they finish, I leave Oliver and hurry backstage to my class. We're the fourth group to perform, and we're dancing to a waltz by Strauss. I find my group already lined up in the hall. I hurry over to Darla and smile at her, expecting her usual toothless grin. Instead, her head is down and she's biting her nails. She whispers that she has to use the bathroom.

I double-check the program order taped on the wall. The class onstage now is almost done, and we only have one more to go before it's our turn.

"Can you do it in less than three minutes?" I ask.

She nods and runs down the hall. I chase after her in case she needs help getting her costume back on. Luckily, there's an open stall. I hear her gasp, and when she comes out, she's crying. She's ripped her shoulder strap and is holding her costume up with her hand.

"Dressing room," I shout-whisper.

We tear out of the bathroom and bolt down the hall. Thank goodness someone's left a sewing kit with safety pins on the dressing table. There's no time for any sewing, so I do a quick fix with a safety pin. At least she won't dance topless. By the time we get back, our class is no longer in the hall.

"Oh no," Darla whimpers. "Did we miss our dance?" She's about to burst out crying again.

I grab her and we run into the dark wings. Our class is lined up there, still waiting. "Whew. We made it," I say as we rush into our places. I joke by wiping fake sweat off my forehead. My hand brushes my glasses, reminding me to remove them. I always prefer performing without them. I'm less nervous when the audience is just a dark blur. I glance over for somewhere to place them. Oliver is still sitting on the metal steps, so I hold them out to him with a questioning look.

"Knock 'em dead," he says as he takes them from me.

I rush back into place and take a deep breath. I *tendu* my right foot and round my arms in first position. A second later, our music begins. I try to count the first notes before we start dancing but get lost. That classical intro baffles me.

I must look panicky because Darla stage whispers the intro counts and then mouths, "Go."

With that, we do our *balancé* steps to enter, which are waltz steps. Onstage, my mind turns off and my body kicks into muscle memory. Luckily, I don't have to perform any double *pirouettes*. I'm pretty confident in the steps, and I get through the choreography without any mishaps. Before I know it, the dance is over.

"That was so much fun," Darla says as we enter the wings. "Thanks for helping me with my costume. It held up great." She gives me a big hug. "I'm going to miss you lots."

"Me too," I say, and I mean it. As she heads to the dressing room, I make my way through the wings to Oliver.

He smiles as he hands me my glasses. "You rocked it."

I grin back. "Thanks." I slip them on and try to look between all the smudge marks his fingers left. "When are you up?"

"Next dance. See you after." With that, he heads around back to reach stage right.

A couple of minutes later, Oliver leaps diagonally across the stage with the three other boys. They perform a pirate dance to contemporary music. The boys jump and turn throughout the dance, and when they finish, loud applause follows. Of course, I think Oliver's the best.

Next, Suzie's class performs to "Le Piccadilly." When she finishes, we hug each other and she reminds me to visit her soon. After she runs off with the rest of her group, I remain in the wings waiting for Alison's dance. Her class performs last, and I can't wait to watch her.

The show moves quickly, and soon Alison's class is lining up in the wings. While they wait, some of the girls retie their pointe shoes out of nerves. Alison catches sight of me and winks. A second later, her face turns serious, and I know she's concentrating.

A few minutes later, the group onstage finishes. As soon as the applause ends and they run offstage, the haunting introduction to "Moonlight Sonata" plays. I hold my breath as Alison rises to pointe and *bourées* onstage with her class. She's wearing a rhinestone headband and a flowy white costume overlaid in ice blue netting. The stage fills with a pool of blue light, Alison glowing at its center. I gasp at the eerie yet breathtaking effect, like finding beauty in the sadness.

I haven't seen the dance before, but I know Alison performs her solo midway through. My heart beats faster as that moment approaches. As soon as she takes command of the stage, my nerves melt away. Her confidence and grace captivate the audience. Her elegant lines are liquid and fluid, filled with emotion.

When she finishes, the audience cheers. Even though I'm not supposed to, I peek out at them. I catch sight of Dad in the third row. He's standing and applauding with a giant smile across his face. If he knew what really happened, I doubt he'd smile like that. I'm glad we vowed to never tell him. He's gone through enough pain with Mom. He deserves some happiness now.

"Come on." Oliver yanks me away from the curtain. "We have to all go onstage now, remember?"

"Oops, I forgot."

I run out to the hall and line up with my class. From out there, I hear our closing music start. Madame Dupree returns to the stage and calls out each class. The older girls line up in the back and the younger classes stand in front. Once we're all onstage together, Madame Dupree announces that she will now hand out the awards.

Awards? I didn't know there would be awards. All eyes go to Louise as she wheels out a table with two gold ballet trophies.

Madame Dupree moves across the stage to the table. "The first trophy will go to the most improved student— someone who has worked diligently from the first day."

As Madame picks up the smaller gold trophy, the students all shoot hopeful glances at one another. I can picture it on my purple shelf. All I have to do is move some books out of the way.

"And the award goes to…"

I bite my lip and hold my breath.

"Darla Valentine."

Darla? My shoulders sink. As I watch her step forward to take the trophy, I think back to her first day. Back then, she couldn't turn without getting sick. Now, she pulls off doubles. I have to agree, she did earn it. I applaud loudly for her, and as she takes her place back in line, I smile and congratulate her.

Madame Dupree lifts the larger gold ballet trophy and continues, "The next award is for the best dancer."

Well, I know that's not me.

"Alison MacAdoo," Madame Dupree announces.

Of course. Who else? But she deserves it also, and I'm thrilled for her.

As Alison makes her way to the front of the stage, she glances back, and we smile at each other. In the audience, Dad stands and applauds.

"But now," Madame continues, "there is still one award waiting that Jeremiah made himself out of blown glass." She motions to the wings, and Jeremiah carries out a glass trophy in the shape of a giant teardrop flanked by a dragon and an eagle.

"Now I'm sure you are all wondering what this award is for," Madame says. "But the fact of the matter is, I cannot tell you."

Murmurs course through the audience and dancers.

"It is a secret award. In addition, I cannot even present it to the student who earned it. Jeremiah inscribed the recipient's name with invisible gold ink. But, I will say this: the student will know who she is in a moment. She is the one who not only saved this school, but also saved one of the students. But for reasons she knows, the recipient and the exact details of this award must always remain a secret."

My breath hitches.

"Who gets to keep it then?" Suzie calls.

Madame pauses until the murmuring in the auditorium quiets. "The award will remain in a locked case in the school."

"Locked? What good is that?" the blond boy says. "It's like an invisible award."

"Yes," Madame says. "But in many ways, that is much better. It's the pride you carry within you, knowing you accomplished a brave feat, far beyond what you thought you were capable of."

My heart swells. I try not to look at anyone and give anything away.

"And with that," Madame says, "we conclude our program."

After the curtain closes, the students head out to the dressing rooms and lobby, discussing the secret award. A few moments later, Madame Dupree makes her way backstage. She nods at me. Her eyes reveal what she can't say in front of everyone.

"Can I speak to you in private?" I whisper.

"Follow me." Madame Dupree leads the way down the hall.

As soon as we're away from everyone, I whisper, "Oliver helped me."

"I'm aware of what happened," Madame Dupree says. "He told me you deserve the credit."

"But—"

"No buts." She places her hand on my shoulder. "Now, what I want to know is, are you returning next summer?"

"I would love to."

"If you work hard next year at your regular dance school, I will take you personally to the Coppelia Shoppe to find the perfect pointe shoes for you."

"Really?"

"Yes, but you must practice, practice, practice."

"I promise."

"Good." She leans down and kisses my cheek. "Until then, I will miss you."

"Me too," I say.

"And speaking of the Coppelia Shoppe, there is someone here to see you. She's waiting in the teacher's lounge. Come with me."

I follow Madame Dupree to a back room. Sitting inside is Madame Babikov.

"I will leave you two together," Madame Dupree says as she closes the door.

Madame Babikov rises from her chair using her pink cane for support. "I watch recital. You did good job."

"Thank you," I say, wondering why she summoned me to this back room.

She sits back down, and with trembling hands unties her child-sized orthopedic shoes. "I show you something." She slips the shoes off and unrolls her black knee stockings. "Look."

I glance down at her bare feet and gasp.

She has no toes.

She gazes at me with sad eyes. "You understand, yes?"

It takes me a moment to put it together. I can hardly believe it. "You mean that rumor was true? You were the one that got away?"

She lowers her head. "I was young—twenty-one. I come here to teach summer class. I meet young man from town. Fall in love. He lie to me… you know rest."

I stand there speechless.

"I want thank you—for put end to madness." She reaches into her purse and hands me a small gift box.

Inside is a necklace with silver pointe shoes. "It's lovely," I say. "But I can't—"

"You must take," she says. "I insist." She stands and clasps it on my neck. "But keep secret for now. Yes?"

I nod. I touch the pointe shoes, feeling their delicate weight against my skin. "Thank you." I hide the necklace under my costume bodice. "And please thank Koshka for me."

"Thank him?" Madame Babikov arches an eyebrow. "Such a tricky old cat. You have secret with him too?"

I grin.

Madame Babikov tilts her head, studying me. "As you wish. I give Koshka your regards. We see you next summer, if fates allow." With a sparkle in her eyes, Madame Babikov shoos me off. "Now go to your family."

As I head into the crowded hall, Alison weaves her way to me, holding her giant trophy.

"It's beautiful," I say as I examine it.

She leans in close and whispers, "It is, but that glass trophy tops this one."

I notice two students eavesdropping, so I nudge her in the side and say, "I wonder who that was for."

While we're talking, friends and families fill the backstage, hugging and congratulating students. Dad emerges between the crowd of well-wishers, his arms full of flowers. As soon as he spots us, his face lights up with a huge smile and he hands a dozen red roses to each of us.

"Where did you get these?" I ask.

"I had them hidden in the jeep." He stares at me a moment. "You look different. Did you get taller?"

"I wish," I say.

"Pride in yourself will do that." Alison gives me a secret wink.

Dad hugs us. "Talk about pride, I'm bursting with it! I know Mom would be too. You girls did such a great job today." He pauses, and his eyes go kind of misty. "She always loved when you two danced."

That lubbly jubbly feeling comes over me and my heart fills with my family's love. I sense Mom's presence with us. I may never become the world's greatest dancer or painter, but I know their love will surround me, no matter what.

As we head out the theater door, Oliver runs over. He's holding a pink and white wildflower.

"Can I talk to you alone?" he asks.

I glance up at Dad.

Dad smiles. "Go ahead."

I follow Oliver outside to the back of the theater, away from the crowd of students and parents. When we get there, he glances around to make sure we're alone.

"This is for you." He hands me the flower, his eyes glinting. "I picked it from the woods."

The wildflower has three white petals with a hanging pink bud. The pouched-shaped flower looks like a ballet slipper. "I've never seen a flower like this."

"Neat, huh? It's called a lady slipper. They grow wild near my cabin. Grandad says they're some kind of orchid."

I sniff it, and as I take in its fruity scent, a fairy pops out. The fairy beams at me and then disappears back into the pouch. I stare at it, then at Oliver.

He shoots me a mischievous grin.

My heart flutters. I know I'll save this flower forever.

"Do you like it?" Oliver's face flushes. "It's the prettiest one I could find."

"I love it." I pause a moment. "But I don't have anything for you."

"You did more than anyone will ever know," Oliver whispers. "And now Grandad and I don't have to move away."

"I'm so glad. I can't imagine you living anywhere else."

We're quiet for a moment. Oliver lowers his head and slips his hands in his pirate costume's pockets.

"So maybe I'll see you next summer?" I finally say.

Oliver lifts his head and perks up. "You bet. I have so much else to show you. *Giselle* isn't the only ballet that comes alive in the forest."

"There are more?" I ask.

"Yup." With that, Oliver leans in, kisses my cheek, and grins. Then he runs off, split leaping deep into the forest.

"Show off," I mutter.

Hugged by the glow of the late afternoon sun, I head back to Dad and Alison, wrapped in a smile I can't erase.

Acknowledgments

A million thanks to my caped-crusading agent, Britt Siess of Martin Literary Management, for championing Kiki MacAdoo from the start with her tireless work and insightful guidance.

I am also eternally grateful to Hannah Smith, Emma Nelson, Olivia Swenson, and everyone at Owl Hollow Press for providing Kiki the opportunity to dance her way into the big world. Additional thanks to M.E.L. Tongol for envisioning the Kiki in my mind's eye and bringing her to life on the book's magical cover.

A special thank you to Dan's Papers and their sponsors for supporting writers on the East End of Long Island. I am filled with gratitude for the opportunities they provided.

To every student I've had the privilege of teaching, thank you for sharing the magic of dance with me. Know that I've treasured every moment. I am also endlessly grateful for all the joyful times with my dancer friends through the years: Susan, Viana, Addie, Danielle, Maryanne, and my personal angel, Sparkle (who always said I should write a children's book). I love you all.

Additional love and gratitude to my amazing mother-in law, Elsie (aka Mom #2), for her humor and never-ending enthusiasm. To my German shepherd, Gracey Valentine, for her spontaneous bursts of love and demands for immediate hugs. And to Jenny, my cheerleader across the pond (whose psychic hairdresser predicted my book would find a publisher!), I send a huge thank you for all of your encouraging words.

My deep heartfelt gratitude also goes out to my uncle Nick and my cousin Bill for helping me through a difficult loss while I wrote this story. I can't thank them enough for their kindness and support after the sudden death of my mother. She, along with my father and brother, always surrounded me with the arts and now all guide me from above. I hope that somehow, they know.

I am also forever grateful to my husband, Nick, who read this story a bazillion times—even though he kept reminding me he wasn't exactly the target audience. I love him and can't thank him enough for his never-ending support and creative insight. Somehow, he always believes in my crazy dreams and helps them come true.

As a final note, I also wish to thank all the frontline workers who are currently putting their lives at risk during the unprecedented pandemic we are facing at this time. You are the true heroes of this world.

COLETTE SEWALL is an award-winning writer who spent the majority of her life as a dancer and studio director. Since she's also worked as a medical assistant, flight attendant, actor, and artist, she believes she's like a cat with nine lives. She is a direct descendant of Samuel Sewall, one of the judges who presided over the infamous Salem Witchcraft Trials of 1692 (which can be a bit awkward when she runs into a descendant of one of the accused witches).

She lives on the eastern end of Long Island with her husband and psychic German shepherd, Gracey, and is in desperate need of more bookshelves. When she's not writing or painting, she's probably perusing one of her favorite libraries or used bookstores.

#KikiMacAdoo
#KikiMacAdooandtheGraveyardBallerinas